SATISFY 2

Once Just Wasn't Enough

SATISFY 2

ONCE JUST WASN'T ENOUGH

LEIGH McKNIGHT

ISBN: 978-0-9725965-0-3

Printed in the United States by Morris Publishing®
3212 East Highway 30
Kearney, NE 68847
1-800-650-7888

S<small>ATISFY</small> 2

O<small>NCE</small> J<small>UST</small> W<small>ASN'T</small> E<small>NOUGH</small>

Secrets can be exciting. . .

Secrets can be fun. . .

Secrets can be everything. . .

Until you get caught. . .

PROLOGUE

Dr. Teyona Carter had her secrets!

A year ago, when she stepped outside her marriage and got caught up in the sexual and dangerous world of the much younger, sexy as hell, badass, Bobby Johnson, she thought she could have her cake and eat it too without anyone finding out. Well, she was wrong! Very wrong! Because there are some secrets, especially the steamy ones, that have a way of not remaining secret for long . . .!

Very often, what's done in the dark does comes to light and her involvement with Bobby Johnson had done just that. Problems began for Teyona when she could no longer betray her husband and tried to end the relationship with Bobby. Unfortunately, Bobby wasn't having that and made it clear that not only was he unwilling to let her go, he had no intention of letting her go. Her refusal to communicate with her young lover led to dire consequences; pictures of her and Bobby, exposing their dirty little secrets. Intimate, compromising pictures of her and Bobby Johnson were delivered to her at home, then later, to her husband's office, alerting him of their torrid several months romance. Once Steven found out about the affair, he ceased all communications with Teyona and moved out of their home and into a hotel. Later, while watching the nightly news and learning her life was in danger, Steven pushed everything else aside and rushed to Teyona's defense.

After he forgave her, she felt she'd been given a second chance and vowed to never allow anyone or anything to interfere in their marriage again. Ever! Evidently Bobby Johnson didn't get that memo! He could've had a buffet of women at his beck and call, but he wanted Teyona! Because he'd fallen hopelessly and senselessly in love with her, he posed a threat to her marriage. Frustrated with the way she'd used him and cast him aside, Bobby decided that if he couldn't have Teyona, his one true love, then no one else would.

Bobby executed his planned vengeance on the same night Teyona and Steven set out to mend their relationship. Enjoying dinner and dancing, they had arrived home and went directly upstairs locked in an ardent embrace while nibbling at each other's ear lobes and talking dirty, promising each other a gloriously hot and passionate night. While Steven sat on the bed undressing, Teyona headed into the bathroom. She was elated; they'd shared another wonderful night and she felt like their marriage was returning to what it had been before her infidelity with Bobby Johnson. She hurriedly made herself up and put on just the right outfit to reward her man for being so thoughtful and romantic and for forgiving her stupidity.

Moments later, Teyona reentered the bedroom wearing a red breakaway bra and panty set and doing a sexy little dance. She was surprised to see Steven in bed, completely covered up. A little disappointed, she teased, "Don't tell me you went to sleep without me. I thought you were gonna wait for

5

me." She danced over to him, sat on the bed and slowly pulled the comforter down from Steven's face. She couldn't believe her eyes. Stunned as shock overtook her face, she noticed as Steven's eyes were slightly closed. His mouth was wrapped with heavy tape. The same heavy tape bound his hands and feet together, rendering him helpless. It took Teyona a minute to wrap her mind around the picture before her but only a moment for her to move.

Slowly, her mind began to work. "Honey," she shrieked, jumping up from the bed. She dropped to her knees and as she frantically began removing the tape from Steven's mouth, she saw a white handkerchief lying on his chest. She picked up the handkerchief which reeked with the distinct smell of chloroform with two fingers. She would never forget that smell after having used chloroform on dozens of frogs in her biology lab classes while in college. Certain of the substance on the handkerchief, she flung it aside. Fear gripping her entire body, Teyona looked around, quickly scanning the room until her eyes connected with those of Bobby Johnson's. He was sitting on the love seat on the far side in the bedroom with his feet propped up on the coffee table, looking completely at home in his surroundings. "What have you done to him?" a frantic scream tore from her throat. "What have you done to my husband?" she yelled at him. Then, sobbing she turned back to her husband. "Steven, baby, wake up." She gently slapped his face, attempting to bring him around. "Steven!

Steven, are you all right? Baby, please be all right!"
She tore the tape from his mouth.

"Move away from him," Bobby Johnson
demanded. Teyona turned and looked at him again.
"I said move away from him!" He repeated.
Slowly, she got up from the floor. "Now, come
here. Don't worry, I used just enough of that shit so
I could tie his ass up. He'll be coming around soon,
trust me! Now, come here!" He lifted his hand to
her, gesturing for her to come to him.

"Why are you in my home again? Why can't you
just leave us alone?" she hurled at him.

"I always knew I was gonna return the favor to
Mr. Tough Guy over there." He nodded toward
Steven. "Especially since he came to my job, telling
me what he was gonna do to me if I didn't leave
you alone." Bobby sat erect on the chair, a smug
sneer etched on his lips. "Did he tell you he came to
see me? Did he tell you what he intended to do to
me if I didn't leave you alone?" His attempt at
laughter came out of his throat sounding like a bitter
grunt, his eyes never leaving Teyona. She didn't
reply. "I just bet he didn't. Well, he told me he
would cut off my balls, stuff them in my throat and
choke me to death with them, and he told me that in
front of the whole damn crew." Teyona could see an
extra supply of anger rising in him. "Imagine that!
That shit embarrassed the hell out of me."

Bobby Johnson looked totally different now than
he did the last time Teyona saw him. No longer was
he the vibrant, fun loving, happy-go-lucky young
man she once knew. He looked older, like he

7

hadn't slept in days, he looked unkempt. Teyona's face involuntarily creased up. She could smell him from across the room. Proof that he'd not washed in several days.

"Come here," he yelled and there was something about the way he sounded and looked at her that time that made her obey.

Teyona walked over to him. "Why are you here, in our house," she gestured with her hands, "meddling in our lives again, Bobby? Why are you here? Why won't you just leave us alone? We don't care one damn thing about you! Why are we so important to you?"

"Because I'm in love with you, bitch! Don't you understand? That's why I'm here," His eyeballs bulging from their sockets as he spoke. "You know I love you. Didn't I tell you that before? You used me for what you wanted then you threw me away like yesterday's garbage. You didn't give a damn about me or what I was feeling, but now, you're gonna pay."

Teyona's voice shook when she asked, "If you leave now and say you'll never come back here, we won't call the police. Our lives can go on as though this little escapade didn't happen."

"You'd like that wouldn't you? Sorry to disappoint you but I got other plan for both of you."

"What are you talking about?" Her eyes piercing into his. "What are you planning to do to us?"

She turned to look at Steven, not wanting him to hear any of what Bobby Johnson was saying. He pulled her from her thoughts when he asked, "You don't know what I'm gonna do?"

"No," she nervously answered a little above a whisper.

"Well, let me tell you. I'm gonna fuck that pussy that I love so much, and I'm gonna do it right here in your house, right there in that bed," Bobby pointed a finger toward the bed. "And when I'm waxing that ass this time, your old man will be watching. When I'm done with you, I'm gonna kick his ass, then I'm gonna cut off his balls and ram them down his fucking throat just like he threatened to do to me! See how tough he is then."

He turned his deadly eyes back to Teyona and terrified now, she said, "Bobby, please! Don't do this! Please! Just leave us alone. Will you please do that? Just go, please."

A smile erupted across Bobby's face. "Oooh, I love it when you beg, baby. That shit turns me on," he said, his eyes lingering on her. Then he turned his attention back to Steven and saw that he was coming to. Bobby said, "She didn't tell you how she loves to beg me for it, huh? Right here under your roof." He lifted both hands in the air. "I bet she didn't tell you that, did she?"

Teyona's eyes darted toward Steven. "Don't listen to him, Steven," she said, then, lifting her hands to Bobby, she asked, "Why are you doing this?"

Teyona saw Steven's face contort as he wiggled, trying to free himself, but she knew that as tight as Bobby had bound his hands and feet together, he'd have to be Houdini for that to happen. In a fair fight, Bobby Johnson wouldn't stand a chance against Steven. Although he was older, Steven was well built, muscular, he was a powerful man. He was physically much stronger than Bobby Johnson. The only advantage that Bobby had in addition to Steven being tied up was that Bobby appeared crazed and there was no telling what he might do.

"What are you worrying about? It ain't gon matter no way. His ass will be dead and if you're not careful and don't get with the program, your ass will die first!"

"You'll never get away with this," Teyona tried talking sense to Bobby. "The police will find out you did this."

"I don't think so. I heard about that little incident you had with that patient of yours. That bitch that went and offed herself yesterday, but I'm sure you know about that. So who's to say that another one of your patients didn't come after you because they had some score to settle?"

"Irene Powell is dead?" For a single moment Teyona had forgotten her own surroundings and again was in a state of disbelief. She had no idea that Irene Powell had killed herself.

"Oh, you didn't know. Well, yeah, the bitch committed suicide in her room in some psych ward," Bobby Johnson spat out.

Feeling defeated, Teyona and Steven exchanged a brief look.

"Look, let's not get off track here," Bobby said, licking his lips and reaching for Teyona. "Let's get down to business."

Teyona moved out of his reach and sneered at him, asking, "What kind of man are you? You have absolutely no compassion for anyone or anything other than yourself. Makes me wonder what's happened to you, why are you so angry at the world?" She looked at him with disgust plastered all over her face.

Bobby paused giving her a dark look. "I don't think you're in no position to talk that shit to me. Why don't we talk about you? What kind of person are you? You were banging me behind your old man's back every chance you got, anytime, anyplace, and everywhere you wanted it, so don't you try to put me down, psychoanalyze me because I don't need those services." Bobby tried to pull Teyona into his arms to kiss her. Bobby's action set Steven on fire. Angrier than he'd ever been, despite his thrashing around on the bed, he wasn't able to undo the tape that bound him. He could only watch helplessly as Teyona tried fighting Bobby off of her before he slung her across the room where she landed on the bed. He followed and landed on top of her. It was then that Teyona felt something hard between their bodies. It was a gun. Bobby Johnson had come into her home carrying a gun intending to use it on her, Steven or both of them. Bobby took Teyona's small wrists into his hand holding them tightly as he pinned them above her head. He used his free hand to run up and down her body, touching her breasts, then between her thighs. He grinned, leering at Steven as his hand slipped under her lacy panties and began caressing her feminine spot. Unable to watch what another man was doing to his wife, Steven closed his eyes and turned his head away.

Driven by love for his wife, Steven snapped his head back to face Bobby again. "Look, man," he began, "do whatever you want to me, but don't do this to my wife. Please, leave her alone!"

Still lying on top of Teyona, Bobby Johnson replied by removing his hand from between her thighs, pulling his gun from his belt and slamming it against Steven's head, causing blood to gush from the open wound.

"Steven!" Her screams were deafening as she struggled to free herself to come to her husband's aid. She writhed frantically under Bobby, too terrified and upset to remember that her movements turned him on. He closed his eyes and threw back his head, grinning and thinking how great it was going to be to feel Teyona's flesh wrapped around his manhood again, holding on to him, gripping him in a way no other woman ever had. He opened his eyes again looking at her with his face drawn into a tight, pensive expression. He lowered his face to hers licking down from her scalp to her cheek. She grimaced, jerking her face away from him and yelled, "Damn it, Bobby, stop it and get off of me, you insane asshole! Get off of me now!" That angered Bobby even more.

12

He turned the gun on her, his face now set in a grim, lifeless expression. "If you don't shut the fuck up, I'll blow your pretty little head off right now! Try me if you think I'm fooling around, you hear?" he said to her. He turned back to Steven again, his sick smile reappearing. "I bet you'd like me to leave her alone, wouldn't you? Well, I will leave her alone as soon as I'm finished with her," Bobby Johnson said harshly before he pulled down the red fabric of Teyona's negligee, exposing her breast. His eyes feasted on them as he ran his tongue over his lips seconds before his mouth covered her nipple, clamping down and began sucking hungrily on it.

"Don't do that man!" Steven's mouth trembled with anger as he yelled, still trying to free his hands as the blood continued to flow down the side of his face from the gash. "You rotten, stinking, son of a bitch. You coward! If you untie me, I swear, I'll fucking kill you and I'll do it with my bare hands. You hear me? I'll fucking kill you."

Bobby was too busy feasting on Teyona's breast to give any thought to Steven and his idle threats.

"I'll kill you, you piece of shit. Untie me, man," Steven demanded.

Bobby reluctantly pulled his mouth from her breast and gave Steven his attention. "Look who wants to throw down! You trying to impress this fine ass mama you got here?" Bobby Johnson taunted Steven.

"Afraid to take me on man to man?" Steven yelled, continuing to struggle violently to free

13

himself. He had to do something otherwise that monster was going to rape his wife and who knows what else to her, right before his eyes. "But you are not a man, are you? No! Not a real man! You are just an immature boy trying to represent himself as a man but you and I both know that you are far from that, don't we?" Steven had to divert Bobby's attention away from his wife.

Bobby looked at Teyona. Shaking his head, he said, "What is it gonna take for me to shut that damn fool up?" He turned back to Steven. "So you don't think I'm a man? I'm gonna show you just the kind of man I am when I'm fucking your girl's brains out." He returned to sucking Teyona's breasts again, fiercely going from one to the other while Steven watched with tears mingling with his blood, streaming down his face.

"Are you afraid to take me on?" Steven yelled, his lip curled in an angry snarl, exposing his teeth.

"You're gonna cause me to change my plans, old man! It looks like I'm gonna have to kill you first, then do your hot little wife, and man she is hot." He looked admiringly up and down Teyona's body.

Bobby Johnson kissed a struggling Teyona hard on her mouth before he crawled off of her.

Recognizing what he was about to do, she screamed, "No, Bobby!"

He ignored her screams and walked around the bed with his gun aimed at Steven's head. "You can say goodbye now, Doc!" he hissed. "Go ahead! Turnover and kiss your beautiful wife goodbye

14

because this will be the last time you'll ever see her," he gloated.

While the young man kept his eyes on Steven, Teyona eased her hand under her pillow, probing until she located the gun that she'd purchased just a short while ago. Not exactly sure why earlier that evening, she'd removed the gun from her closet, loaded it and placed it under her pillow, but at that moment she was grateful she had.

Getting up from the bed, she aimed the gun at Bobby Johnson. "Bobby," she called out. "Drop the gun and move away from my husband!" she ordered, Bobby turned to look at her but kept his gun trained on Steven. "I said drop the goddamn gun and move away from my husband, you son of a bitch!" Teyona commanded. "If you think I won't blow your head off right where you stand, you are out of your fucking mind. I am sick of you and your shit. You've come into my home again and again to fuck with my family. You were told to stay away from us but you won't stop. You gotta have it your way. Well, this is one time too many. I am done having you control my life. I ain't having it no damn more. Do you understand that?" Tears began to fall down her face and the gun shook slightly in her hand as she talked. "Please, don't do this," Teyona begged through tear swollen eyes.

It was at that moment Bobby acted as though he'd lost his damn mind. . .

CHAPTER 1

TEYONA AND RACHELLE

Water poured down Teyona's tall, curvy, honey colored body. After a while, she twisted off the shower, stepped out and after toweling off and rubbing her favorite scented lotion over her body, she slipped on a navy thong. She ran a brush through her long auburn hair pulling it up on top of her head into a bun with several tendrils falling about her face. Her complexion was smooth and creamy and her features; small and keen, a perfect fit for her absolutely gorgeous face. She applied mascara, a little blush and pink lip gloss. After hanging a pair of gold earrings in her lobes, she slipped her feet into navy red bottom strappy four inch heels. Then, she stood in front of the full-length mirror in her bedroom. Satisfied with how she looked in the navy classy, exotic Gucci dress that landed a couple inches above her knees, showing off her gorgeous shapely legs and curvy body, she grabbed her keys and purse and left her house. Outside, she climbed into a white late model Mercedes and after buckling her seat belt, she headed downtown to the Marriott Hotel where her friend, Trudy's art show was being held.

It was late August and though it was almost eight o'clock that Thursday evening, it was still bright and sunny, with a slight breeze floating in the air. The weather wasn't the only pleasantry. The traffic flowed smoothly and the clock on the Benz's dash showed Teyona she'd arrived at the event ten minutes early. She walked up to the double glass doors of the hotel that were eagerly opened for her by a young, handsome doorman dressed professionally in a black suit, tie and a crisp white shirt. She stepped into the cool, elegant and beautifully furnished lobby and strolled up to an attendant who directed her courteously to a bright chandeliered lit room that held extravagant looking art sculptures and paintings. The room was dotted with several tropical plants and aquariums strategically placed around the room to enhance the ambience. An array of beautifully dressed and cultured patrons mingled, eating hors d'oeuvres and drinking champagne served to them by waiters dressed in black slacks, white shirts and jackets.

Moving further into the dazzling room, speaking to other patrons and accepting a glass of bubbly from a waiter, Teyona checked her watch while searching the room for Rachelle, her best friend, who had agreed to meet her there. Teyona clicked her teeth and shook her head. Just like Rachelle, she sighed, finishing off her champagne and stopped a passing waiter for another glass. She was getting impatient. Rachelle was always late for everything but for tonight's event, she'd hoped Rachelle would make an exception and be on time or at the least arrive soon, with Trudy scheduled to enter at any minute to speak to the crowd and answer questions

17

about her art pieces. More people were streaming into the room now and Teyona watched the entrance for Rachelle.

Another waiter presented her with some hors d'oeuvres which she gracefully declined before returning to scan the now crowded room for Rachelle with her impatience quickly turning into anger and disgust. Didn't Rachelle know how important this night would be for Trudy? Still scanning the room, she mentally ran through all the things she would say to Rachelle when she saw her. She smiled wryly. She had some choice words for her friend when suddenly her eyes flew wide open and the champagne glass slipped from her hand crashing loudly on the floor at her feet sending shards of broken glass and a splatter of liquid spilling across the polished hardwood floor. All activity inside the room halted. Frozen in her tracks, Teyona became the center of attention and within moments, a waiter was at her side with a viselike grip on her elbow. She blinked while taking a deep, measured breath to steady her nerves. Upon opening her eyes again, she frantically scanned the crowd for the familiar face that had been so upsetting to her in the first place, but she didn't see him. Surely he couldn't have vanished. Or, could her eyes be playing tricks on her, she wondered.

The waiter signaled for housekeeping and a young woman in uniform arrived and began to clean up the glass and champagne from the floor.

"Are you alright, miss?" the waiter asked Teyona, who appeared to be devastated by whatever she'd seen. He held onto her elbow to support her while he looked in the direction where her eyes were canvassing. Not noticing anything out of order, he returned his attention back to Teyona. "Miss, are you alright?" he asked again.

Teyona had tried for months to erase past mistakes from her mind but here they were again, front and center in her brain. For a while she didn't say anything as her eyes darted around the room. Then, she looked at the waiter and nervously replied, "Oh yes, I'm fine. Thank you. I thought I saw someone I once knew."

Still holding onto her arm, the waiter, glancing around again, asked, "Can I get you anything? A water perhaps?"

"No, I am fine," she replied, scanning the room again to see if she could see the person she thought she'd seen earlier or at least Rachelle.

"Are you sure?"

"Yes," she assured him. "Thank you very much."

With that, the waiter released her arm glancing back at her as he walked away.

It wasn't long before Trudy was escorted into the room. A round of applause rang out as she greeted and thanked everyone as she made her way up to the podium to begin to talk about her work. As Trudy spoke, Teyona found it difficult to concentrate on what she was saying. She kept turning her head to survey the room throughout Trudy's remarks.

After the speech, Trudy began answering the attendees' questions. Halfway through the question and answer portion, Rachelle arrived. Immediately upon seeing Teyona, she walked up behind her and with her mouth close to Teyona's ear, whispered, "So, what did I miss?"

Teyona nearly jumped out of her skin, quickly turning to see Rachelle standing next to her. Rachelle was beautifully clad in a black split-neck, exposed zip fit, flare dress that clung to her small waist and settled a little above her knees. Her high heel shoes and clutch purse were black and her jewelry was silver and expensive. Rachelle, a beauty like Teyona, was also in her forties, didn't look nowhere near her age. Her cinnamon hued complexion was smooth and creamy and required minimal makeup. Her lips were full and shapely, her nose was small and her large, dark eyes were surrounded by long, thick lashes. Her high cheekboned face was draped with thick, sable hair that hung in soft curls over one shoulder.

Rachelle had recently received a huge salary increase when she was promoted to Human Resource Director from Human Resource Manager at a large insurance company where she now garnered a six figure salary. She had become depressed with the office politics at work and in response had gained a ton of weight which led to her taking a one year sabbatical to go live with her mother in North Carolina. At the end of the year when she returned to Columbia and work, it didn't take the administrators long to reinstate her in

Human resources and promote her. Rachelle was now back to her normal weight, looking fabulous and ready to wreak havoc in someone else's life. "You didn't tell me you and Steven are on the cover of Black Enterprises Magazine this month," Rachelle beamed at her friend. "You guys are doing the damn thing. Congratulations." Then her facial expression changed. "I wish George and I had something that we could share, something that we agreed upon."

"Why are you always late?" Teyona snapped, not addressing Rachelle's comment. "Can I ever count on you to be on time for anything?" She demanded.

"I'm here now," Rachelle laughed off Teyona's scolding that wasn't unusual. For as long as either woman could remember, Rachelle always showed up at an event after Teyona and they just laughed it off but recently, Rachelle was always arriving late.

"You were supposed to be here at 8 o'clock. Where have you been?" She was annoyed and it showed.

Her feelings were not lost on Rachelle who leaned away from Teyona and looked at her. "I had a few errands to run and I got held up but what's wrong with you? You look as pale as a ghost."

"Nothing is wrong with me," she quickly tried to brush the subject aside. "I just thought you'd want to be here in support of Trudy. When I asked you two weeks ago about coming, you assured me you'd be here."

"I am here," Rachelle joked.

"You know what I mean." Teyona sighed.

Rachelle rolled her eyes and said, "You still haven't told me what wrong with you. What's got your panties in a bunch?"

"I told you, nothing is wrong with me. I just hate it when we make plans and you show up late. I don't know whether you've noticed it or not but you're late almost all the time now. What's up with that?"

"No, I haven't noticed but like I told you, I had some things to take care of and it took longer than I'd intended but relax girl. Get that stick out of your ass. I'm here now." Rachelle turned, lifting a glass of champagne from a passing waiter's tray, took a sip and looked at Teyona again. "You sure you're okay?"

Teyona gave Rachelle a sour look, not wanting to lie again in answer to what had her so upset. And, Teyona was upset! Very upset! But she didn't want to talk about it there.

Rachelle changed the subject. "You look fierce, girlfriend."

Teyona looked Rachelle up and down. "You don't look so bad yourself," she replied.

"You want to have some dinner after this is over?"

"Yeah, I guess so." Teyona began to settle down. "I see our husbands couldn't join us tonight."

Rachelle waived a hand dismissively, "I knew George wouldn't be here because of other commitments but what happened to Steven?"

Taking another sip of champagne, she asked, "Another late night at the office?"

"What else is new?" Now it was Teyona's turn to waive a hand dismissively. "Steven said if he could get away, it would be towards the end but if he wasn't able to make it, that I should spend no more than $10,000."

Rachelle let out a low whistle and put her hand on her hip. "Since when does Dr. Steven Carter put Dr. Teyona Carter on a budget or should I say an allowance?"

Teyona shrugged, "I guess he had to do something due to my overspending over the last year. I really went overboard with my spending. It was my way of handling my depression. And not a good way for our finances, I might add," she said, accepting another glass of champagne from one of the ever present waiters circling the room before taking a sip.

"I understand," Rachelle said, glancing over at the door and placing a hand on Teyona's shoulder. "Well, it really does look like we're on our own tonight."

"Like I said, what else is new?" Teyona said with a little smile.

Later after talking briefly with Trudy and congratulating her on her one woman show, Teyona and Rachelle both purchased art pieces, and after leaving their addresses for the pieces to be shipped to them, they left the hotel and headed to The Cheesecake Factory on Harbison Boulevard for dinner and drinks and later, perhaps they'd hit a club and do a little dancing. As Teyona followed Rachelle to the restaurant, she kept checking the rear view mirror. After parking their cars, they got out and walked into the restaurant together. After they were seated at a table draped in a rich burgundy tablecloth, Teyona ordered lobster, a baked potato and a green leafy salad while Rachelle ordered grilled salmon, asparagus and a salad. Both ordered a glass of red wine. Their server placed water and a basket of breadsticks on their table.

Rachelle had barely lifted her glass of wine to her lips to take a sip when Teyona blurted out, "I saw Bobby Johnson tonight."

Rachelle began to choke on her wine, spilling some down the front of her dress and on the beige tablecloth. She snatched up the burgundy linen napkin that was spread across her lap and dabbed the wine from her mouth and her dress. Her eyes were bright with concern. "What did you just say?" she coughed out, incredulously, as she continuously dabbed her napkin on the tablecloth to absorb the spilled wine.

"I said I saw Bobby Johnson tonight." Then, Teyona clarified her statement. "Well, it wasn't actually Bobby Johnson. We know it couldn't have been him but I saw someone at the art showing tonight who looked exactly like Bobby. He was more polished from what I can remember, but exactly like him."

Perched on the edge of her seat, questions flew from Rachelle's mouth. "You saw someone who looked like Bobby Johnson? Exactly like him? Are you sure?"

"Yes, yes and yes I am." Teyona was emphatic.

"Now I see why you were so freaked out earlier." Rachelle settled back in her chair and took another sip from her wineglass.

"Can you blame me?"

"Well, no. I'm sure I'd be freaked out also had I seen someone who looked like that monster," Rachelle admitted, then she shrugged and added, making light of their conversation, "Well, they say each of us has a double."

Teyona's gaze locked on Rachelle. "You are acting really nonchalant about this."

"No, I'm not," Rachelle defended.

"You are too."

"What do you want me to do? We know what happened to Bobby and whoever it was that you saw tonight, you know it wasn't him. There's no way that he can ever hurt you again," Rachelle said and Teyona's mind returned to that awful night when Bobby Johnson came into her home with the intention of killing both, her and Steven.

"I wonder what that person was doing there," Rachelle wanted to know. "Did he approach you? I mean what happened to him? Did he leave before I arrived?" The questions continued to roll out of her mouth.

"I don't know who he was or what he was doing there. No, he didn't approach me and I don't know what happened to him. One minute he was there and the next, he was gone."

"How did you happen to notice him? What was he doing when you saw him?"

"I don't know." She was clearly frustrated. "He was just standing across the room looking at me."

"And he didn't approach you or try to say anything to you?"

"I told you no. As I said before, Rachelle, he was just standing across the room, looking at me. It was chilling, the strangest thing I've ever experienced."

Rachelle shook off a shiver that ran through her body. "That must have really been unnerving to say the least."

"Tell me about it."

"I wonder who that person was," Rachelle pondered, stroking her chin.

"So do I. Seriously, the resemblance was uncanny."

"Did Bobby ever mention having any family here in town?"

"We didn't talk much about family. That wasn't the nature of Bobby and my situation." Teyona looked thoughtful before saying, "Although he did mention once when he wanted to spend a holiday with me and when I told him to spend it with his family as I would be doing, he said he didn't have family. I took that to mean that he was alone in the world but I didn't question him further.

Rachelle stared at Teyona intently for a second before she said, "We hadn't talked about Bobby Johnson in nearly a year."

"Yeah, I know. What are you getting at? He's not anyone that I want to talk about. I want to forget

26

everything that I know about that character," Teyona said, shaking her head.

"Don't take this the wrong way, but do you ever think about him or you know, miss him and what the two of you shared?"

"Bobby Johnson and I had sex! That was all that we shared! Nothing more!"

"Apparently that wasn't all it was for him and certainly that's not all your involvement entailed because as it turned out, you shot and killed the man."

"Do you think you need to remind me that I killed that man? You don't think I've thought about that night every single day since it happened?"

"I just wondered. No big deal."

"Frankly Rachelle, I am offended that you would ask me something like that."

"I know, but just answer the question."

Teyona sat in silence for a moment. She wondered why her best friend would suddenly be so insensitive of her feelings. What brought that on? Because she cared so much for Steven, was she upset that Teyona had cheated on a man as wonderful as him? When Teyona thought about it, she couldn't believe that was it because Rachelle's husband, George, was a wonderful man by all standards and she didn't have a problem cheating on him. Teyona finally admitted, "He has crossed my mind on occasions but it's never in a way that I want him here to get involved with him again. I mean I do wish he was here and that what happened to him didn't happen, but I don't think about ever being with him in a sexual way. That was the worst mistake of my life and I promised myself and my husband that I would never betray him again and I mean that."

Rachelle chuckled.

"Did I say something funny?" Teyona asked. She was still on edge. And just having a conversation about Bobby Johnson caused a strange stir throughout her body, but it was not in any way sexual.

"My laughter has nothing to do with Bobby Johnson. I was thinking about how you have been boasting about how Dr. Steven is bringing it to the sheets these days." Rachelle whistled. "The man has become the long distance, power runner and has given a sista her groove back."

Her words caused Teyona to offer a slight smile. She was glad that Rachelle had put an end to their conversation about Bobby Johnson. "Yes, I have to say things in our bedroom are better than ever." Teyona beamed. "That man is giving it to me like some untamed, magnificent beast and I am lapping it all up." She stopped talking briefly to stare out across the room. Then, she returned her attention to Rachelle. "Although, for a while there, Steven acted like he didn't want to touch me and when he did, he would either hurry as if he wanted to get it over with or he'd just revert back to his old ways of not satisfying me."

"Really?" Rachelle asked, shocked.

"After that awful night, there were times when I would look up and see Steven staring at me. I couldn't tell whether he was disgusted with me or simply hated me for what I had done. I didn't know. I just knew the look on his face wasn't pleasant. Even now, although he said he forgave me, I'm not sure that he has."

"Of course he has forgiven you. Tee, we all make mistakes. None of us are perfect. So don't read too much into everything. I'm sure Steven has forgiven you and has moved on."

"I can only hope so."

"Of course he has. You said he's bringing it even better than before. Do you think he'd be able to handle you with such passion if he were still holding onto some animosity from the past?" Rachelle asked, then answered her own question. "I don't think so, my dear. You know how men are. If they're really pissed at us, more often than not, they don't want anything to do with us until that anger blows over."

Suddenly a thoughtful wrinkle creased Teyona's brow.

"What is it?" Rachelle inquired, leaning across the table, staring at her.

"I don't know what you're talking about." Teyona pondered a thought, "but I know for a fact that there were times when Steven and I would be intimate with each other and I imagined something from the past would run through his mind and he would treat me as if he were trying to hurt me."

"Details."

"It's as though he's unleashing his fury on me, something evil and while he's plunging into me for all he is worth, he's glaring, unsmilingly into my eyes. It's so intense that sometimes it frightens me."

With a huge grin on her pretty face, Rachelle gave her body a little shake causing her breast to jiggle as she reached her hand across the table to Teyona. "Oh yeah? Give me some." She gave Teyona a high five. "Umm, fierce! That just makes the whole thing that much better. I love all that intensity, that raw, mind blowing, nasty ass pain. Child, if you don't like that, Felicia bye." Rachelle waved one hand in the air and rolled her eyes as she lifted her wineglass to her lips and took a healthy swallow. "Hell, let George be mad at me and see if I care. To tell you the truth, for that very reason there have been times when I've purposely made him mad just before we went to bed so that he would be turnt up and go at me unmercifully." Rachelle laughed heartily.

"What?" Teyona joined in the laughter. "You're kidding me."

"I kid you not. When George goes to bed angry at me and we make love, that is one night of guaranteed, glorified, great sex."

The two women chuckled.

"You are one crazy broad. You know that, don't you?" Teyona said and when they stopped chuckling, she took a deep breath and shrugged her shoulders. "It's wonderful that Steven and I are back on track, and I couldn't be happier."

"Considering all you two have been through, it seems you both have settled into a good place." Rachelle lifted her glass. "Cheers to moving forward." Teyona lifted her glass and they toasted. "And congratulations again on your and Steven's most recent accolades. The Power Couple of the South! That's so great."

Teyona smiled. "Thank you."

They were on their second glass of wine when Rachelle noticed that Teyona's eyes were dark as she glanced around the restaurant.

"What are you looking for?"

"I don't know. I'm still a little jittery I guess."

Rachelle stared at her friend. "Girl stop! It's that over active imagination of yours playing tricks on you again as it did earlier tonight." Teyona gave her a peculiar look and she added, "I'm just saying. Even if you do think you saw Bobby Johnson's double, it is understandable that you would have all these emotions running around inside your head. Hell, not so long ago, you experienced a traumatic situation, something that could have been tragic for you and Steven, something no one in their right mind would want to go through."

"It wasn't my over active imagination, Rachelle. I know what I saw, besides, I am a therapist and I am trained to see a situation for what it is. I am supposed to be in control of my *over active imagination*, as you call it," Teyona said and added, "I don't know who that man was but he was definitely there. He looked identical to Bobby Johnson and he sure as hell scared the shit out of me."

"I knew something was wrong with you," Rachelle said as she brushed a piece of hair behind

31

her ear. "Why didn't you tell me when I first got there?"

"I don't know, a little pissed off with you I suppose," sharing her feelings, Teyona added. "You've been missing in action lately. You didn't show up at the club last night after we made plans, Rachelle." They had made plans earlier that week to meet at one of the country clubs that they were members of and frequented. "I tried calling you first at home but I got no answer. I even tried your cell but you didn't answer that either. What's up with you lately? You are not having an affair on George again, are you?"

Rachelle leaned back in her chair, rolling her eyes. "Oh here we go with that shit again."

"What else am I supposed to think if you keep coming up missing when we have plans for a girls' night out and I am left alone because you didn't show?"

Rachelle laughed off the comment. "I had every intention of meeting you at the club but last minute, George came up with one of his bright ideas. He wanted to see this movie."

"A call would have been sufficient," Teyona said and asked, "Which movie did you see?"

"Child, I don't know. I think it was that last racing movie that Paul Walker made. You know the one that Tyrese is also in. Fast & Furious 7, I believe, but before the coming attractions were finished, I was asleep." Rachelle laughed, causing Teyona to laugh with her.

After a moment, Teyona asked, "Would you mind terribly if we didn't go dancing tonight?"

"You never miss an opportunity to go dancing." Rachelle took a sip of wine. "Girl, you'd better get that man out of your head. Bobby Johnson is dead and you don't ever have to worry about him again, so quit making yourself miserable."

"I know, but it was just earth shattering seeing someone who looked so much like him."

"I'm sure it was, but you know it wasn't so let's move on from that."

Shortly afterwards, Teyona and Rachelle left the restaurant and headed home.

Less than thirty minutes later, Teyona pulled her car into their three car garage next to Steven's Hummer. She wondered why he bought that vehicle. He never drove it, hardly ever touched it. He had someone keep it clean and shiny though. Other than that, the truck wasn't touched. If he didn't drive his Porsche, he drove the Benz. That Hummer was just an untouchable toy for Steven, Teyona had thought. She shut off the engine, got out of the car and entered her house through the elegant, state of the art kitchen that was a combination of granite counter tops, polished stone floor and stainless steel appliances. She turned on the ceiling light, dropped her purse and keys on the granite island top and flipped on lights as she went through the house. With the thought of Bobby Johnson or someone looking like him invading her thoughts again, Teyona felt uneasy and was certain to check all the doors to ensure they were locked before going up the hand-carved staircase to take a shower and change.

Returning downstairs in a black negligee, matching sheer robe and slippers, she made a cup of herbal tea that she took into the den with her. She turned on the flat screen TV mounted on the beige wall that was a perfect contrasting compliment to the deep brown couch and matching chairs in the huge room that had large deep windows, heavy beige ceiling to floor drapes and French doors leaving to the terrace. The coffee and lamp tables were glass and chrome with lamps made of polished nickel base and hardback fabric shades. Expensive framed portraits hung on the walls and large tropical plants were placed around the room.

Teyona set her tea cup on the table and settled deep into the couch where she intended to wait for Steven to come home. As she sipped from her tea cup, she flipped through the TV channels but was oblivious to what popped up on the screen. Finally, as she leafed through a magazine, she settled on a news station. Steven was putting in more hours now than ever and came home late almost every night but tonight, he was unusually late coming home.

After watching the news and Steven still wasn't home, Teyona tossed the magazine on the table and went upstairs to bed.

CHAPTER 2

RUSSELL

Russell arrived at the Columbia Metropolitan Airport in Columbia, South Carolina, from Detroit, late Wednesday afternoon. He'd come to Columbia before to check into a family matter and after not finding anything significant in the six weeks he spent there, he'd returned to Michigan. He'd been surprised when he started his investigation into the man's activities, that he didn't uncover anything negative. It appeared he was a very hard working man who was dedicated to his patients, after which, he went home to his wife. Now, three months later, Russell returned to complete his investigation and this time, he would not leave until he had all the answers he needed and the situation resolved.

He grabbed his bags from the conveyor belt, rented a car and drove to a nearby hotel where he checked in, picked up a copy of The State Newspaper and took the elevator up to his room. Upon entering the room, Russell threw his bags and newspaper on the bed. The cream colored room was spacious with a sitting area to include a couch, chairs, tables, lamps and plants, the beige curtains were drawn and bright sunlight filtered through the large windows.

Russell opened one suitcase, removed a manila folder, a copy of Black Enterprises Magazine and scissors and carried the items and the newspaper over, laying them on the coffee table in front of the couch near the window. He walked up to the windows. Looking out over the city, he took several deep breaths as he ran a hand up and down his jaw line in deep concentration. After a moment, he purposefully turned away from the window, walked over to the mini-bar and poured Scotch over ice cubes in a glass. He took two gulps from his glass before he walked over and picked up the manila folder from the table. He took one more gulp from his drink before he set the glass down on the table and dropped down hard in the chair. He flipped open the folder, removed an envelope containing pictures that he spread out on the table along with a note pad and pens. He picked up the newspaper and began to examine it. Picking up the scissors, he cut out several articles and pictures, placed them on the table with other pictures and tossed the newspaper in the trash can near his chair before picking up the Magazine from the table.

He read the caption across the top of the magazine cover. 'COLUMBIA'S NEW MEDICAL POWER COUPLE.' Below the caption, was a picture of a man and woman along with an article that read, 'Columbia's newest medical power couple of the South recently opened medical clinics in Charleston, Greenville and Charlotte and handpicked physicians to run the day to day operations. . ." Russell's eyes moved back to the faces of the couple pictured there. His brows knitted as he studied the woman, running his thumb over her face. He hated to admit it but staring at her caused a peculiar slow heat to creep through him. What was it about her that had struck him so profoundly and shook him to his core? The spark of desire was unmistakably instant and incredibly real. Irritated, he frowned and shook his head to clear it of the thoughts that had begun to consume him. He let out a long frustrated sigh, then slammed the magazine back down on the table and kicked the chair near him, sending it sailing across the brown carpet to where it crashed against the wall. Russell closed his eyes, laid his head against the back of the couch and covered his face with his hands. A sudden weariness came over him, no doubt from lack of sleep, and more than likely, suppressing his regret about the years of not resolving the issues with his brother before he was so violently taken away from him.

Again, Russell's eyes glanced at the couple on the magazine cover but he concentrated on the woman's face. He released another deep sigh and bending at the waist, with his eyes closed, he pressed his forehead in his hands. When he opened his eyes again, he gazed at the woman and wondered why he couldn't erase thoughts of her from his mind.

Moments later, Russell picked up the scissors again and cut the picture from the magazine cover and several pictures from inside the magazine before throwing the magazine away. He picked up a pad and pen, sat back on the couch and for the next thirty minutes or so, he made notes. When that was done, he checked his watch. Nine fifteen in the evening. He scooped up the pictures, articles and notes into an envelope that he slid into a folder, got up from the couch and placed the folder into one of the drawers that he covered with some clothing that he removed from his suitcase. He pulled from his suitcases a change of clothes that he laid on the bed, then going off to take a shower, he knew exactly what he had to do. "And, someone is going to pay," he vowed.

After toweling himself dry, Russell threw the damp towel across the shower rod. Standing naked in front of the bathroom mirror, he splashed aftershave on his face and neck and brushed back his short black wavy hair. Russell was tall and handsome; medium brown complexion, mesmerizing hazel eyes, nice shaped nose over full shapely lips that could break into a smile that could melt your heart and take your breath away. His body had muscles bulging in all the right places and biceps a living Adonis would kill for.

Returning to the bedroom, he stepped into a pair of white boxer briefs, pulled denim jeans up thick, muscled thighs, over trim, taut hips to a tight six pack waist. He left the top two buttons open on the short sleeve white shirt that not only exposed a bit of his broad, hairy and muscled chest but powerful corded brown arms. He stuck his bare feet into a pair of black loafers, then armed with his cigarettes, lighter, cell phone and keys, he left his room. As he drove around, he thought it odd that he still couldn't get the woman's face from the magazine out of his mind.

Coming upon a Red Lobster on Two Notch Road, he pulled into the parking lot, got out of his car and entered the crowded, well lit restaurant. Once seated, water and a menu were placed on the table. Russell hadn't eaten since breakfast but he hadn't realized how hungry he actually was until a seafood platter, leafy salad, breadsticks and sweet tea were placed on the table before him.

After having a second glass of tea, Russell left a tip, paid his bill and exited the restaurant appreciating the pleasant breezes that greeted him, a stark difference than the soaring temperatures when he left the hotel. He was exhausted driving back to the hotel but decided to stop in at the hotel lounge for a drink before going back to his room to crash. He entered the dimly lit, semi-crowded room and looked around. People were mingling, jazz music played in the background, and cigarette smoke floated through the air. The bar was lined with people but Russell spotted an empty table and was making his way across the lounge when he was approached by a gorgeous dark complexioned, medium height woman who looked as though her spectacular body was poured into the black mini dress she was wearing.

"Hi," she greeted him, a friendly, sexy smile on her face, her eyes moving from his handsome face down his incredible body. "The atmosphere in here just improved more than one hundred percent," she said.

"You don't say," he glanced down at her.

"Oh yeah," the sultry, dark hair, striking woman, said. "Take my word for it,"

Russell's eyes darted toward the vacant table again. "Hey, why don't we grab that table over there? It seems that's the only one available."

"Why don't we," the woman agreed, linking her arm with his while walking with him across the room. He held out a chair for her to sit, then walked around and took a seat facing her. "I'm Journea, by the way."

"Russ," he said.

"What are you up to tonight, Russ?" She asked.

"Nothing much," he shrugged. "I stopped in for a drink before turning in."

"Before turning in? You sound as though you had a long and busy day."

"You could say that."

"What are you doing here at the hotel? Are you from out of town?"

"Yes. Detroit. I'm here on personal business. What about you?"

"I'm from Austin, and I'm here for an IT conference."

"IT. That's a great field. How long are you in town for?"

"I leave tomorrow. My conference ended today. What about you? Are you in town for a while or are you leaving soon as well?"

"I really don't know. I just arrived today but I should know something in a few weeks."

"May I ask what is it that you do?"

"I'm an investigator of sorts."

"Ahhh, that's sexy. Who are you investigating?"

Russell gave her a look from across the table. "You know that's not how we roll."

"I know you can't share that information."

"Say, what would you like to drink?"

"I'd love a Margarita."

Russell signaled a waitress, she came over and he placed their drink orders. "So, are you staying here at the hotel?"

"Yes." She gazed into his eyes.

Russell glanced around the room before returning to meet her gaze again. "What did you have in mind for tonight? Hitting a couple of clubs and get your little party on?"

"Up until a few minutes ago, I didn't have anything in particular in mind." She smiled suggestively at him.

Recognizing that look, he said, "I take it your conference went well."

"Yes it did," she replied reaching across the table placing her hand on top of his. "Why don't we get out of here? Your room or mine?"

Russell's eyes popped wide open. He'd never had a problem getting women in the past, but this was a little quick even for him. "I'm game," he smiled across the table at her. "Sounds like a good idea to me."

Just then their waitress arrived with their drinks. Russell handed her a couple of bills and with Journea's hand in his, they carried their drinks as he pulled her through the crowd toward the bank of elevators. They entered the elevator and the doors hadn't completely closed behind them before he pressed the button to his floor, jerked her roughly against him and spun her around, pinning her against the wall. His mouth came down hard on hers. She was soft and warm and as he inhaled her intoxicating scent that completely washed over him, quickly sending enormous heat to his loins, as they continued the kiss, all he wanted to do was get her into his room, out of that dress, into his bed and taste her some more.

He tore his mouth away and gazed down into her eyes. He sunk his mouth down to meld with hers again, thrusting his tongue deep inside her waiting, welcoming mouth, with hot, blazing sweeps. She moaned in his mouth and within seconds, she matched his rhythm and his passion and dueled right along with him. As their kissing intensified, her body began to move against his, slowly at first but quickly building into vigorous gestures. Her hands seemed to be everywhere simultaneously, caressing his shoulders, trailing down to the small of his back, his thigh, his buttocks that she gripped hard, pulling him further into her. Spasms of ecstasy erupted through Russell when Journea's hands boldly clutched his male hardness. Her sharp gasp at the enormity of his erection caused him to move his legs apart so that she could touch him where she couldn't stop herself from touching him. If the elevator doors didn't soon open so they could go to his room, she would drop to her knees and take what she wanted right then, right there and nothing would stop her. This young woman with the angelic face and devil's body was definitely on a mission. The look on her face told him without question, that she was going to take what she wanted from him and there wasn't a damn thing he could do about it.

As if on cue, the elevator doors eased open and they stumbled out still holding onto their drinks, each other and still kissing, making their way to Russell's room. He fumbled in his pocket for his room key card. Upon entering the room, Russell released her, took a huge gulp of his drink as did she before he took her drink and set both glasses on the dresser. Eyes locked, Russell began to unbutton his shirt. He wasn't at all surprised after Journea lowered the zipper and stepped out of her little dress, that she was completely naked except for the four inch stilettos.

Both completely naked now, they moved into each other's arms like magnets tumbling on the bed with Russell on top and between her legs. He kissed her mouth some more before he moved down to her breasts. His tongue alternated flicking and circling the swelling, chocolate pebbles before his mouth enclosed on her breasts, going from one to the other, teasing, kissing, nibbling, sucking, even taunting but giving her undeniable pleasure. She began to whimper like a wounded animal from the assault his mouth, tongue and teeth unleashed upon her, the sensation he evoked inside her. As her whimpers grew into moans, then groans, before he could react, she wiggled out from under him maneuvering on top of him slamming her tongue inside his mouth and whipped it around mating with his. Tearing her mouth away, she looked at him with pure wicked passion in her eyes. Straddling him her tongue traced over his nipples before her mouth opened to nibble and suck on them. Bringing about an intense fire in him, her mouth moved further down his body, creating a wet path down his chest, his abs pausing shortly to toy with the indented navel core. Then, she went on to feel his course pubic hair on her face. Taking his erect penis in her mouth she began using her tongue circling around and around, up and down the shaft. Delighting in the exquisite sensations of Journea's expertise, Russell exercised ungodly will power to not deposit everything he had inside him into her mouth.

Knowing her way so well around a man and his penis, Journea moved her mouth away from him and slithered up his body, the best male body she'd seen in her entire life, the kind of body any girl would want to go to sleep with every night and wake up to every morning. Face to face, gazing into his eyes, she reached down between them, finding what she was searching for, took his heavy male organ into her hand, inserted it at the entry of her vessel then slammed her body down hard on it, evoking a loud gasp from him. She began to buck on him, thrusting against him, twirling on him, taking him into her, deeper and deeper into her hot, juicy canal. She thrashed her head from side to side and around and around with her long dark hair slapping against his face, something that in an odd way, turned him on. As she continued to bring her skills to his bed like a slick new piece of machinery, he moved underneath her, hips gyrating, thrusting upward battling this sultry vixen. Without separating, they changed positions. On top of her now and staring into her eyes, he began to plunge into her with powerful thrusts, in and out, around and around, faster, harder, deeper, at a force that bordered on savagery.

With all the pleasure this woman evoked in him, a woman so willing, so eager to please, why wasn't he enjoying what she was so freely giving? Why couldn't he get out of his mind the face of the woman on some damn magazine cover, the same woman whose pictures were splashed across newspapers throughout the country, someone he didn't even know? Looking into Journea's face, he didn't see her. The face that stared back was the woman he'd seen in magazines, newspapers. That's who he was screwing! The woman he hated! Yet he couldn't stop himself as he plunged almost uncontrollably into her.

Russell and Journea continued their sexual dance, pausing several times to pull in deep breaths only to repeat the cycle that went on until the early morning hours. Shortly after ten that morning, he flicked her hair away from her face, kissed her forehead and nudged her out of a sound sleep. He swung his legs over the side of the bed, reached for his underwear on the floor and put them on. He glanced down at Journea who was pouting, clearly upset that they wouldn't be spending more time together. She was a gorgeous girl. Really beautiful to look at, fun to be with and she was the ultimate fuck, but he had other things to do and time was of the essence.

CHAPTER 3

TEYONA

Teyona had devastated her husband, who loved her unconditionally, providing her with a lifestyle that most would envy. Yet, she did loved and adored him. He had satisfied all her wants, all her needs, except the one she wanted and needed the most. Steven didn't satisfy his wife sexually, and after years of pretending he did while listening to her girlfriends boast about the way their men brought mind bending sex to their sheets, Teyona was left feeling envious and wanting more for her love life. That was what made it tolerable for her to betray her husband the day Bobby Johnson entered her home to repair a bathroom leak. Not only did he repair the leak, he'd awakened something in Teyona that her husband hadn't in the twenty plus years they'd been married, something that'd lain dormant inside her much too long. Bobby Johnson had awakened her entire existence to what sexually satisfying a woman was all about. He'd touched her spirit, her very core. He'd unleashed the most indescribable pleasure on her and though she couldn't deny the guilt that consumed her every time she thought of him, she also couldn't deny being with him, even if it had been only for his sex.

Every inch of him had satisfied every inch of her! Artfully! Astonishingly! Thoroughly!

For several months Bobby Johnson had been Teyona Carter's secret and guilty pleasure until their relationship had been exposed, leading up to a terrifying night where Bobby Johnson ended up dead on her and Steven's bedroom floor.

Teyona winced thinking about that awful night. Bobby acted as if he had lost his damn mind. He swung the gun on her and pulled the trigger. Simultaneously, Steven kicked as hard as he could knocking Bobby's arm up in the air as the bullet left the chamber of both guns. The bullet from Bobby's gun landed in the ceiling, but the bullet from Teyona's gun struck Bobby in his neck and he fell to the floor with a heavy thud.

She dropped her gun to the floor upon seeing that Bobby wasn't moving and that his gun had fallen away from him to the floor. She rushed around to the bed and removed the tape from Steven's hands. As soon as his hands were freed, they were in each other's arms, kissing each other through their tears.

After removing the tape from Steven's legs, he got out of the bed, walked over to where Bobby Johnson lay on the floor and examined him. The bullet had ripped through the younger man's jugular, killing him instantly. Steven went back over to Teyona, and holding her in his arms, he dialed 911. A short while later the police and the coroner arrived, they looked around the bedroom and took statements from Teyona and Steven, before departing with Bobby Johnson's body. That had been the worst night of her life and she had no one to blame but herself. All that had happened was definitely a lesson learned. She knew she'd never behave so foolishly or selfishly again, sacrificing the love of a wonderful man and her family to satisfy some personal itch.

Several months later, after that horrific incident, Teyona returned to her thriving family therapy practice. She hoped that she and Steven's relationship would return to what it was before their world completely fell apart. She saw patients and assisted them in feeling better about themselves, bringing some order to their lives and moving forward in a positive way, only she wasn't certain she had the ability to do the same for her own life. She did know she did everything she could to move that process along.

CHAPTER 4

RUSSELL

On Tuesday evening, Russell drove into the Richland Medical Center parking lot and cruised around, finally finding a space to park. He noticed several cars in the lot but he kept his eyes on the one that was parked in Dr. Steven Carter's designated parking space. Russell checked his watch. Ten thirty-five. After shutting off the engine and releasing his seat belt, Russell stretched out his legs, reached into his jacket pocket and pulled out a pack of cigarettes and lighter. He plucked a cigarette from its pack, placed it between his lips and lit it. He inhaled deeply and released a stream of smoke from his mouth and nose. He cracked the window in his car for the smoke to escape and rested his head against the seat with his sight still fixed on the building, hoping something would turn up tonight. Sitting and watching these clowns go on with their lives without him learning anything significant was getting old.

After a while, Russell frowned, blew out a frustrated breath and checked his watch again. Eleven twenty. He lifted a elbow, just as he was about to take another drag from his cigarette, he noticed the door to the medical building open;

a man dressed in a dark suit and a woman dressed in white, exited the building. They waved good night to each other, went in different directions to their respective cars and drove out of the parking lot.

Within fifteen minutes, Russell saw who he knew, from previous investigation and photographs, was Dr. Steven Carter, walk out of the building, carrying a jacket across his arm and a briefcase in his hand. Russell leaned down in the seat of his car so that he wouldn't be noticed but was able to watch as Dr. Carter climbed into a navy sedan, started the engine, fasten his seatbelt and drove away. Making sure that Dr. Carter was out of the parking lot, Russell then switched on his car, fastened his seatbelt and with the lights out, he followed Steven out of the medical center and didn't put the lights on until he merged with the night traffic. For almost a half hour, Russell followed Dr. Carter. He watched him turned into the driveway of a massive house in an upscale section of Columbia, get out of his car and enter the house before heading back towards his hotel.

CHAPTER 5

TEYONA

"Get off me, Bobby!" Teyona screamed. With her heart pounding against her chest, she kicked and pushed frantically, trying to shove Bobby Johnson's powerful, muscular body off of her where he had her pinned on her bed.

As angry tears streaming down her face, she yelled, "Stop it, damn you!" Teyona began to claw at any portion of Bobby's flesh that she could fasten her nails into. But he'd been so intent on getting what he wanted, what he needed from between her golden thighs that he didn't notice she'd drawn blood from him with her long manicured fingernails. As Teyona opened her mouth to cry out again, Bobby Johnson enclosed her mouth with his, more to taste her mouth, suck on her luscious lips then to muffle her screams. He'd wanted Teyona from the first moment he saw her. He wanted her now, and nothing was going to stop him from claiming what he knew he couldn't live without.

Bobby grabbed Teyona's wrists and with one hand, pinned them above her head to the bed, then he pushed his tongue into her mouth, trying to elicit a response from her. She knew she had to stop him.

She tried to force her body away from him, trying to free herself, but she was no match against Bobby. The more she wiggled underneath him, the more it turned him on, making him more determined to have her. Bobby used his free hand to pry her legs apart before wedging his body between them. Feeling the tip of his engorged member brushed against the entry of her vagina, she used everything in her feminine arsenal to prevent what she knew was inevitable from happening. But, she was fighting a losing battle. And though she screamed, punched, kicked, bit and clawed him, he was unfazed. She was powerless to stop Bobby Johnson from having his way with her. He was relentless, liked a craze animal in his pursuit. He was going to have her and in the next moment, he claimed what he wanted most when he slammed his huge swollen cock into her, causing her to let out a blood-curdling scream, "Bobby."

Suddenly, she rose in her bed, her body covered in perspiration and shaking violently. That scream had sucked all the air out of her lungs. She took a couple of deep breaths as her eyes frantically searched her semi-darkened bedroom illuminated only by the shaft of light filtering from the hallway through an ajar door. As her eyes came to rest on her husband sleeping soundly in bed beside her, it was then that she realized that it was all a dream. Or rather a nightmare! Bobby Johnson wasn't there! He wasn't trying to rape her! Bobby Johnson was dead! And, she had killed him!

Teyona released a long shuddering breath. This was one time when she was grateful that Steven was a sound sleeper because there was no way she could've explained to him why she'd awakened in the middle of the night screaming the name of another man, the man she'd had an affair with and had shot dead in her bed almost a year ago.

Shaken from the nightmare, Teyona threw back the covers, eased out of bed and after removing a fresh nightgown from a drawer, went over to the bathroom door, glancing over her shoulder to see if Steven was still asleep before she entered and closed the door behind her. She hit the light switch flooding the huge opulent bathroom with soft light. The walls were pale yellow and white, the room contained double sinks, commodes, marble counter top and flooring and a basket of mixed flowers, mostly white and yellow mums sat between the double sinks on the vanity.

Teyona pulled the wet nightgown over her head, dropped it in the hamper, then turned on the cold water over a sink, pulled a wash cloth from the towel rack and after dampening it she pushed the damp hair back on her head and ran the cool wet cloth over her face, neck and down her arms to remove the perspiration before she slipped into the gown.

Calming a little, Teyona hung the towel back on the rack. She picked up a glass from the vanity, filled it with water from the sink and as she lifted the glass to her lips, she stopped suddenly, catching a glimpse of herself in the mirror over the sink. She looked horrible. She'd been frightened, more frightened than she'd been in a while. After a moment, she lifted the glass to her lips and drank most of the water before placing the glass back on the vanity and leaving the bathroom.

She walked across the massive bedroom over to the windows, pulled back the drapes and peered outside at the stillness except for an occasional automobile passing by. At that hour, the only things alive were the trees that moved ever so slightly from the gentle early morning breezes and the lights that lit the streets in the upscale neighborhood.

One month after the incident with Bobby Johnson, Teyona and Steven bought an elegant 4,200 square foot house on Lakeshore Drive. The house had five bedrooms, including two custom designed master suites with showers and whirlpool tubs in the bathrooms; a sun room, a mahogany library, formal dining room, two fireplaces, one on each floor, beautiful heavy carved moldings, walk-in closets and a state of the art kitchen. The floors were hardwood, some carpeted while others were handmade polished bricks and stones. One of the main features of the house was the rear terrace that over looked a pool to one side and a picturesque pond on the other, surrounded by beautiful, colorful flowers.

Before moving into their new home, they got rid of all of the furniture from the previous house. What they didn't sell, they gave away. They were excited about their new home and the neighborhood where they looked to have a fresh start. They didn't want anything in their new home, their new life that would remind them of her affair with Bobby Johnson and what heartache, shame and terror her actions brought to their marriage, family and friends.

For several months after Bobby Johnson's death, Teyona had had nightmares a couple of times a week before the nightmares suddenly stopped. Now, the nightmares were back. She'd not wanted to share with Steven what was happening because her affair with Bobby Johnson had affected Steven far more than she had initially thought. Since the night of the shooting, she noticed that Steven had become quieter, he'd begun drinking more and there were times when she'd catch him staring at her with an odd look on his face. Steven had said many times that he'd forgiven her but she knew that somewhere deep inside that he hadn't nor had he forgotten, and she didn't blame him. She wasn't sure that had the shoe been on the other foot that she would've forgiven him or forgotten the situation either.

After a while, Teyona walked away from the window and returned to bed. As soon as she pulled the covers up over her chest, Steven turned over in bed and nestled close to her back.

"Are you alright?" he asked, stretching an arm across her.

Her mind tried to conjure up a true answer that wouldn't upset her husband, but she couldn't. "Yes, I just had to get a drink of water," she lied as her eyes stung as she fought back tears, tears because she'd lied to her husband again, regardless that it was a small lie. The last thing she wanted was for Steven to worry about her. He was a wonderful man, husband and father and a conscientious doctor. Putting in long hours caring for his patients as he did his family and when he was at home, she wanted him to have complete peace of mind and get the rest that he needed. Teyona turned in bed and softly kissed her husband on his forehead. "I'm fine, baby. Now, go back to sleep. You need your rest."

Within a few minutes, Teyona heard the heavy breathing that let her know that Steven had gone back to sleep. As she lay awake next to him, she glanced over at him and couldn't help how her stomach twisted in sympathy for him. She knew how devoted he was to everything he did and he didn't deserve what she'd done to him. If she had it to do over again, she'd never betray him as she'd done. It was then that Teyona allowed tears to flow down her cheeks. She cried for her past sins, vowing yet again to never fall into a similar situation.

That Friday morning, she set plates of grits, scrambled eggs, turkey sausage, toast and a pot of coffee on the table. Sitting across from her, Steven appeared tired, nervous, which matched exactly how Teyona was feeling. When she looked up to ask a question and saw him staring oddly at her, she asked, "What is it, honey?"

"What do you mean?" Steven glanced down quickly directing his attention away from his wife to a piece of toast he took from the plate and began spreading strawberry jelly on.

57

"I just thought you were looking at me in an odd kind of way," she said, hoping he didn't hear her screaming out Bobby Johnson's name last night.

"Are you imagining things again?" He asked, taking a bite of his toast and jelly.

"Oh, I don't know. It was like you had something on your mind that you wanted to say to me." Teyona lifted the coffee pot from the table and filled each cup with the steaming liquid before setting the pot back on the table.

"No, I don't," Steven replied, scooping up grits and eggs with his fork before placing the fork into his mouth and taking another bite of toast. "If I was looking at you a certain way, I wasn't aware of it."

She looked at him as she added cream and sugar to her coffee. "Okay, I just asked."

"You never did say where you wanted the picture hung that you bought at Trudy's art show the other night."

"She was disappointed you couldn't make it, by the way."

"It couldn't be helped."

"I explained that to her," she replied as she cut a piece of sausage and forked it into her mouth. "About that piece of art, I was thinking we could hang it above the table in the foyer. What do you think?"

"That's a good spot for it."

Before they finished breakfast, Teyona was certain she saw her husband giving her several more odd looks. She didn't know what to make of it and she didn't ask again.

CHAPTER 6

STEVEN

On the way to work, Steven's mind returned to the conversation he and Teyona had at breakfast. She was right to say he was looking at her in an odd way because he was. He knew she felt he was still trying to decide whether he had forgiven her for the affair she had. That may have been a part of it but it was mostly him wondering whether she'd noticed something different about him; the way he treated her, responded to her, the way he made love to her. He felt a little guilty because he knew of the affair Teyona had had with the young man who nearly destroyed their lives but she hadn't known about a number of affairs he'd had, the most recent was a two year relationship he'd just ended weeks ago with one of his nurses who was married with children.

Steven arrived at work just before eight thirty. His office was already lined with patients of all ages. After donning his white medical jacket, his nurse brought his first patient in and handed him a chart. "Thank you," he said to his nurse. "Hello there," he greeted a nine year old girl whose mother brought her in, complaining of a sore throat. "How are you this morning, Mrs. Goodman?" he said, acknowledging the mother with a smile. "Why don't you come over here, Lizzie? Get up on the table and let me take a look to see what's going on with your throat," Steven said softly to the girl who left her mother's side, walked over to him and he helped her up onto the bed. "There are a lot of bad bugs going around so we can't take any chances. Okay," he said as he sat on a stool at the side of the examination table. He reviewed the chart then he rolled up closer to his patient and said, "Okay now, open wide and say ahhhh."

Lizzie obeyed and about ten minutes later, Dr. Steven Carter wrote out a prescription that he handed to Mrs. Goodman. "It's nothing serious, no temperature or aches. It appears to be simple allergies but this script will help to ease those symptoms. She should be just fine," he said and returned his attention to Lizzie. "You had a good summer, Lizzie?"

"Yes, I did, Dr. Carter."

"That's great. How's school?"

"Fine."

"Great." Then he bit on his bottom lip in pretend concentration. "Are you studying hard? You know you have to study very hard and focus to achieve the goals you want, right?"

"Yes, doctor."

"That's a good girl. I can see you're going to do just fine." He patted her shoulder. "Keep up the good work, okay?"

"I will, doctor."

After Mrs. Goodman thanked the doctor, she and Lizzie left his office.

At two that afternoon, Steven had his receptionist order in lunch. He quickly ate a chicken salad sandwich, followed by a glass of sweet tea and immediately went back to seeing patients. He saw his last patient at five-fifteen. From there he went to Palmetto Richland Hospital to make rounds and didn't arrive home until after ten in the evening.

"Oh, there you are," Teyona said, getting up from the couch where she'd been reading a file and having a glass of ice tea when Steven entered the den. "Would you like a drink?"

"Yeah," Steven said, coming out of his jacket that he dropped on a chair, loosened his tie and sunk down in the couch.

"Rough day again?" Teyona asked, placing the drink in his hand.

He took it, turned it up to his mouth and took a huge swallow. "Just more of the same." He took another swallow of his drink.

She sat beside him on the couch and ran her fingers along his temple. She heard a soft moan escaped him and smiled. "Have you had something to eat or can I heat up a plate for you," she offered.

"I haven't eaten anything since lunch." His hand went up to massage the side of his head, then asked, "What you got?"

"There's some baked chicken, a little potato salad and sweet peas."

"That sounds good. I think I will have some, but just a small portion though. I don't want to be up all night." He gave her a small smile.

Teyona nodded in understanding. "I'll be right back." She got up, went into the kitchen and moved around to fix a plate and heated it up in the microwave. Steven reclined into the cushions of the couch and massaging his temple, he tried to relax. Within minutes, Teyona returned to the den, carrying a tray with the plate of food, a glass of iced tea with lemon and a napkin, setting the tray on the coffee table in front of Steven.

"Thanks, babe," he said as he scooted to the edge of the couch and began to consume his dinner. "How was your day?" He asked shoving some potato salad into his mouth.

"Interesting." She took a seat next to him on the couch.

"How so?" Steven bit off a piece of chicken, picked up the napkin and wiped his mouth.

"I saw a young lady today, first time patient, a lovely young girl but she's a cutter." She reached up and touched the side of his face and ran her fingers along his beard.

"Oh really?" Then he uttered, "Umm." He turned his face so that his lips gently brushed her hand. He always loved it when she mingled her fingers with his beard. "How did that go?"

"It was sad, but I could tell she wants help, she wants something better for herself."

"That's positive." He took a sip of tea.

"Yeah. She really is in a low place in her life but you know," she began and took a deep breath, "sometimes it doesn't matter how low they've sunk, you can still see a desire to change, to make something better of themselves. I see that in this girl."

"That's a good sign. As long as she wants the help, is willing to accept it and does the work, then I feel sure she should be alright."

"Absolutely."

Steven nodded. "I always believe that you are the very best at what you do. But, talk to me about it."

She removed her hand from his face and drawing one leg under her, she shifted so that she could look directly at him. With a thoughtful expression, she began, "From what she's told me, she had a history of neglect, abuse; both mentally and physically at the hands of her own family, the people who are suppose to be closest to her, the people who are suppose to protect her. Well, they didn't protect her, she was abused on a number of levels and as a result, she went into a deep depression. While in high school she somehow fell in with a group, a young man in particular, and she believed that this was going to be a fresh start for her. It worked out really well there for a while; the young man said all the things she wanted and needed to hear and did all the things she wanted to have done. She thought she had died and gone to heaven. All that changed and came crashing down on her one day when she found him in the arms of another girl. She was devastated, more than she was before and she found herself turning to drugs to soothe her devastation, her pain. When the drugs didn't work or when she couldn't come up with enough money to supply her needs, well, that's when the cutting began. She told me watching that knife go over her skin and seeing the blood momentarily took away all the pain, depression and she felt free." Teyona lifted her head and stared into space.

"That is a tough situation but the important thing is that you don't see her circumstances as hopeless. You believe you can help her. That's a huge part of the battle right there?"

She took a sip of tea. "I hope so. I sure am gonna try," she said, her voice trailing off in a whisper.

A short time later, Steven got up from the couch. He reached for Teyona, gently took her soft, delicate hand in his and she inhaled a deep, soothing breath as they went upstairs. Coming out of the bathroom, she found Steven already in bed. He reached over and threw back the covers for her. That was when she noticed he was completely naked. She couldn't help but smile and as soon as her body touched the bed, he began kissing her and pushing her nightgown up over her head. Tossing the gown aside, Steven pulled Teyona atop him and kissed her again; deeply, thoroughly, passionately. His hands had felt so darn good moving up and down her body. He pulled his mouth away from hers and asked, "Are you still happy being married to me, baby?"

Teyona pulled her face away so that she could look into his eyes. His gaze met hers with a dark, piercing look, one that still took her breath away after being married all those years. She tilted her head to one side, and said, "Of course, I am, honey. Why would you ask that?"

"I don't know."

"You don't ever have to question that," she replied and threw his question back at him, "Are you happy being married to me?"

"You know that I am. I love you, Teyona."

She pulled him close and held him tightly. "I love you too, Steven," she whispered, her eyes closed and tracing the features of his face with the tips of her fingers, pausing at the beard that she knew she would never grow tired of. His beard was one of her greatest weaknesses. He took a deep breath and inhaled her scent, a scent that was uniquely hers. His mouth came down hard on hers again and her tongue shot inside his mouth. The kiss was full of want, need, passion. It was primal. Regardless what had happened in their lives, together they were man and woman, husband and wife and they were on fire for each other, always seeking, exploring, driving each other insane with desire.

Steven's mouth moved from Teyona's down to her breasts where he took her breasts into his hands, placed one swollen nipple into his mouth and teased and sucked on it, then he moved to the other and his mouth clamped down hard and he sucked hungrily on it, then back and forth, he sucked on them both,

65

causing his name to escape her lips in a long continuous moan. As he moved down her body planting wet kisses along the way, she parted her legs wide open and in the next moment, he opened his mouth and claimed her intimate spot. He licked, nibbled, then he teased her with his tongue a while before he began to feast on her most intimate spot. She clamped her hands on his head, holding him there, giving him all he was seeking and taking satisfaction in all that he was giving her.

After a while, he moved up her beautiful, smooth body. When their bodies were aligned, she held her breath in anticipation and without opening her eyes, she reached down between his legs and for a moment, caressed him there, enjoying the feel of the length of his massiveness in her hand. He entered her, completely filling her with his manliness, his bold thickness, moving in and out of her, she lifted her legs high up around his waist and squeezing him ever so tightly as she held on and rocked with him, meeting his forceful thrusts. With each surge of his flesh into her, she matched his moves with staggering moves of her own. Then with one last plunge, they exploded simultaneously, satisfying each other as never before. Afterwards, wrapped in each other's arms and without withdrawing from each other, they slept.

In the morning, Steven glanced at the clock on the nightstand. It was seven o'clock. He could hear Teyona downstairs preparing breakfast. He threw back the covers, strode into the bathroom and rubbing his hand along his jaw, peered out the window. Though there had been the threat of rain each day that week, it hadn't happened. The weather report last night had again indicated rain today. Well, we'll just have to see, Steven thought, because he was all set to go to the club that afternoon to play a game or two of tennis.

Steven showered, shaved and dressed in a dark brown suit and a crisp white shirt. He went downstairs to find his wife dressed in a long white clingy robe. Greeting each other with a soft, gentle kiss, they sat at the table, extended their hands to say blessings and began to eat the delicious meal of omelets, turkey sausage, toast and mixed fruit along with orange juice and steaming, hot coffee as they chatted through breakfast.

After breakfast, they went off to work. Steven began his day as usual; one patient after the other throughout the day. His last patient left at five thirty so did most of the staff with the exception of one nurse. Sitting behind his huge mahogany desk, he noticed that the rain had kept its promise today. It was pouring outside. He grinned. Looks like there will be no tennis today, he thought. He picked up the phone and placed a call. Moments later, Abby, his nurse, floated into his office with a huge smile on her face. He gazed up at her. Abby was a gorgeous thirty year old woman with a face that only a short while ago could've earned her an enormous amount of money modeling or representing some cosmetics company. She was five feet, nine with long, shapely legs. Her long blond hair framed a small oval face with large twinkling blue eyes, a thin, pointed nose and bee stung lips that were begging to be kissed.

Abby closed the door, locking it behind her and while never taking her eyes off Steven, she walked over to his desk. His gaze narrowed as he watched her move around behind his desk. He eased out his seat as she moved directly into his arms and held her tightly. At first her lips gently touched his, then running her tongue around his full, warm mouth she was happily rewarded when Steven's mouth captured hers in a burning and passionate kiss that she welcomed and accepted hungrily. He slid his large hands around her slim waist to squeeze her more firmly against him. She parted her legs and arched into his embrace so that he could connect more intimately with her. As the kiss intensified, his grip intensified, grinding his hips vigorously against her as she grinded hard and seductively against him.

She tore her mouth from his and in one wide sweep, she cleared Steven's desk, sending everything on his desk crashing to the floor. She turned back to face him, giving him a devastatingly wicked look. He lifted her atop his desk and quickly moved between her parting legs, taking her mouth in another passionate kiss. She reached down, unzipped his pants and pushed them along with his boxers down his legs. After kissing some more, she extricated herself from his powerful grip, hopped off the desk and kneeled on the floor in front of him. She took his steadily swelling manhood into her hands and boldly staring up into his eyes used her tongue to circle the tip of him several times before taking him into her mouth and began doing unimaginably delicious things to him. While her mouth continued to bear down on him and squeeze him, he closed his eyes, his head rocked back on his shoulders and moved from side to side as he enjoyed the insane act being performed on him.

Catching his first release, she got back to her feet. He unbuttoned her white blouse and reached around her to unhook the white lacy bra exposing porcelain skin and creamy white ripened mounds. He couldn't help but take a moment to appreciate what he saw. Her breasts were round, plump, inviting. He closed his eyes briefly and took a deep breath, appreciating breasts that were pure perfection. He couldn't wait to taste them. First, he buried his face in them before hearing her gasp when his mouth covered one rosy, erect nipple while his hand teased the soft, delicate skin of the other. For a while he sucked one breast while caressing, gently squeezing the other.

Abby lay back blissfully on the desk as Steven dropped to his knees. He pushed up her skirt, snatched her white lacy thong down her legs, leaving it hanging on one high heeled foot. He lifted her legs over his shoulders and his mouth went to her core and began to move against her in a series of kisses, nibbles, licks, triggering waves of pleasure in her. He began sucking on her tender, sensitive, pulsating button, moving his mouth fiercely around every inch of her feminine spot, eliciting moans and groans for she could no longer control herself. She screamed his name over and over, "Steven, Steven," as she parted her legs wider and moved her body against his mouth maddeningly. As he continued to feast on her, she thrashed her head from side to side as moans came from deep in her throat. When kissing was no longer enough, Steven got up from the floor, kicked out of his pants and lowered his body between her thighs. She wrapped her arms tightly around his neck and lifted her feet up on the desk so he could have complete access to her. He entered her with a groan of satisfaction slamming his huge erect penis into her as she thrust her hips up to meet him. He began to move his hips and before long, they were caught in the same rhythmic dance, a dance filled with so much passion, passion that began building inside her and quickly spreading throughout her, fusing their bodies to a point where it was difficult to tell where her body ended and his began. She buried her face in his neck and began to suck and bite him there as he continued plunging into her, faster, harder, deeper with her matching his every single movement. The intensity of their sex rose as her nails dug into his back. They soared to the highest peak and in the next moment, they shot over the rainbow together.

Afterwards, they perched on the edge of his desk. "I don't know why it took us so long to get here," Abby said, glancing over at Steven.

"To be honest, I don't know how we got here today," he replied.

"I don't either but now that we are here, what are we going to do about it? I mean, are we going to go back to our professional roles with all this underlying sexual tension that I'm sure we're not going to be able to ignore."

"Abby, it's like this. I'm married and I'm in love with my wife...."

She interrupted him, saying, "Doctor, you might think you believe what you just said but there's no way you could've made love to me the way we just did if you are so much in love with Dr. Carter. There must be some fracture in your life at home."

Steven exhaled loudly. "I believe two people can have a connection with each other without it having any bearing on what the other might have at home or elsewhere," he began and went on to say, "What I was trying to say before is that I do love my wife, I love her very much but I can also have other interests without it affecting her." He gave her a knowing look. Returning that look, she smiled at him, reached over and gave Steven one final kiss before she scooted off the desk.

Later, after pulling herself together, Abby exited the building through the side door near where she parked her car. Steven stood in the doorway until she was safely in her car and he waved as she drove away. He made some notes in some files, checked his calendar to see what the next day's appointments looked like, and he closed the book. Moments later, he turned off his desk light and walked over to the door. He lifted his jacket off the hook behind the door, picked up his medical bag and left the building through the front door.

CHAPTER 7

RUSSELL

Russell watched Steven as he exited his office, got into his car and drove away. Again, he followed Steven all the way home, watched him get out of his car and enter his house before he turned around and headed back to the hotel.

The next morning, Russell awoke before the crack of dawn. He stretched and yawned, rubbing sleep from his eyes before sitting up in bed, flipping open the manila file he left on the side of his bed and began reviewing the notes he'd written. He separated articles and pictures, putting them into piles and clipped them together. He'd been in Columbia almost four weeks now but it seemed more like four months. He'd done additional checking into the background of several people who he'd previously investigated and though nothing significant had turned up, he wasn't giving up. He still had a lot of work to do. He'd do at least one more sweep on the people whose backgrounds he'd already looked into to see what their stories were but there is one other person whose mind he was definitely going to get into. He was saving the best for last.

At ten that morning, he was still reviewing and making notes when there was a knock at his door. "Housekeeping," came a voice from the other side of the closed door.

Russell put his notes down on the bed. He hopped out of bed in his shorts, rushed to the door and flung it open, surprising the two young housekeepers who were there to tidy up his room. "Morning," he greeted them with a smile.

"We're here to take care of your room, Sir," one housekeeper said.

Russell looked back towards the bed, then returned his attention to them. "If you'll just leave some towels, everything else can stand until tomorrow."

"That's fine, Sir," the other housekeeper said.

Towels were brought in, trash was removed, the housekeepers left, and Russell walked back over to the bed to resume what he was doing. He continued working until his stomach began to rumble. He checked the time on his phone, returned all the information to its folder, and after a long hot shower, he pulled on a brown shirt, blue jeans and brown laced up shoes. He drove to IHOP where he had a late breakfast of French toast, scrambled eggs, bacon and sausage, orange juice and coffee.

While enjoying his breakfast, he couldn't help this lingering thought in his mind that there was something small in his investigation that needed looking into. It may not be anything significant but he had to check it out just to be sure. His motto was and always had been was to never leave any stone unturned. After breakfast, he drove over to the Colonial Life Insurance building. Russell got out of his car, walked across the parking lot and took the elevator up to the fourth floor where he made some inquiries. Leaving that office, he called over his shoulder, "Don't do anything until you hear further from me." He returned to his car, made a notation in his file and said, "Check," before he put his notes away, started up the engine and drove off.

His next trip was to the Medical Building on Taylor Street. He noticed that the sky was getting dark and since there was the threat of rain again, he turned into the underground parking lot of the building and parked. He got out of his car, spoke to someone as he entered the building and studied the board next to the elevator. He saw the name of the doctor he was looking for and took the elevator to the third floor. He had called the doctor's office on his way over, learning she was away from the office but would be back at three. He checked his watch. It was two thirty-five. He opened the door to Dr. Teyona Carter's office and noted that a number of people were waiting to be seen. Success. Everything he'd read about Dr. Carter as far as her accomplishments, appeared to be true.

He walked up to the receptionist desk with the name Meghan engraved on a gold plate on the corner of her desk. "May I help you, Sir?" she asked.

"I've got a bit of an emergency situation and I was wondering whether I could see the doctor today?" Russell asked.

"Have you seen Dr. Carter previously?"

"No. New patient." Russell wanted to have Dr. Teyona Carter arrive in her office and come face to face with him. He wanted to blow her out of the water! After all, she was that bitch who killed his brother! His twin brother!

"Dr. Carter never turns away a patient," the receptionist began and didn't appear to want to stop talking about the doctor as though she was some kind of saint, "but I don't believe she'll be able to squeeze you in today because she was called away, she is running a little behind and has got all these patients to see. I would love to set up something for you tomorrow. Although she's got an extremely busy schedule, if you need to see her, I am sure she will make a way to see you. Can you come back tomorrow?"

Just that one conversation, if Russell didn't know better, he would feel differently about Teyona Carter. He wasn't going to forgive her for what she did to his family because he knew that she was wearing a facade for the public which was so contradictory to who she really was. She could not deceive Russell because he knew the truth about her. She was a chameleon, a tigress who changes her stripes for spots. She could be that wolf in sheep's clothing for the public but he saw her for the wolf that she was and he'd make her pay. Those were simply his thoughts nothing more. Still, if in reality this woman was as perfect as she appeared, he had to find out what drove his brother to her. No, he shook his head violently; he knew what drove his brother to her because she was that kind of woman. She was sexy, gorgeous. She had those incredible good looks that men would die for. But, Russell had to find out what was it about Bobby that would cause a woman like her to welcome him into her perfect life, her perfect world. What would drive a woman like that to his brother? "Why don't I call you back a little later if I can't get something else to work out today," Russell said before leaving the office.

When he got into his car and was about to start the engine, he saw her! In all her glory! Dr. Teyona Carter! "Soon, Miss Lady. Soon," Russell vowed as he watched her walk away from her car and entered the office building.

From what he'd learned so far, both of the Carters appeared to be hard working people, closer to perfect than anyone he'd ever met. Perhaps Dr. Steven was as he appeared, all principled and was cheated on by his wife, the woman he adored but Doctor Teyona. She was definitely the proverbial snake in the grass. Plain and simple! Russell started his car and drove away.

CHAPTER 8

TEYONA & RACHELLE

"What are you doing after work today?" Teyona asked, Rachelle.

"Nothing, really. Probably just a quiet dinner at home with George," Rachelle answered and asked, "Why? What's up?"

"I need to talk with you. When can we get together?"

Sensing the urgency in her best friend's voice, Rachelle said, "We can do it tonight, if it's that important. My house or yours?""

"I'm overdue for a good spa treatment. Why don't we meet at Southern Girls?"

"That sounds wonderful. I'm due one myself. What time should we meet?" Rachelle asked.

"I was thinking around seven. Is that good for you?"

"Yeah, that's great for me but are you sure that's good for you? I don't ever remember you leaving your office before eight at the very earliest."

"I've put in a special request to Meghan that she gets me out of there no later than six thirty and you know Meghan," Teyona said of her receptionist and office manager. She'd been with Teyona since she restarted her practice five years ago. "Girl, Meghan will get it done."

They chuckled.

"Yeah, you've trained your little bulldog well," Rachelle chuckled some more.

"She certainly takes good care of me."

"I'll give her that. So seven it is."

Teyona and Rachelle arrived at Southern Girls Spa on Forest Drive promptly at seven o'clock. They embraced each other before entering the facility and were immediately taken into a room where they removed their clothing, slipped into thick, fluffy white robes and were presented with a complimentary glass of champagne prior to getting a deep tissue massage.

Face down on their tables, Rachelle glanced over at Teyona, giving her the side eye and asked, "So what's got your panties in a bunch this time? You're not having another affair, are you?"

Teyona gave her friend a scathing look, saying, "Girl, no, I'm not having another affair. Are you out of your mind? Didn't I tell you that I would never be that foolish again? Well, I meant it, besides," she smiled shyly, "Steven is fulfilling all of his husbandly duties and then some."

"So he's rocking and rolling with it on a regular now, huh?"

"Rachelle, honestly speaking, had Steven been handling his business like this before, there would never have been an affair to speak of."

"Are you seriously saying sex with Steven now is that much different, that much more amazing than it was all those years ago?"

"That's exactly what I'm saying," she said, as a thoughtful look crossed her face. "I know how that sounds and we've had this conversation before but honestly, Rachelle, Steven is the man. I've told you how well endowed he is." She playfully used her hands to demonstrate the size of her husband's sex organ, "well, he really knows where to put it and how to put it where we both get the most pleasure. Rachelle, I really don't know why it took Steven so long to give it to me the way he's giving it to me now. It is amazing. Steven is giving me mind bending, toe curling sex every night." She whistled softly. "Just when I think he'd done it all, the man comes with something new and different, and I love it. But listen to this. Remember when I told you he would come home late at night, completely exhausted and would go to sleep and make love to me in the morning? Well girl, he's not waiting until morning anymore. That man is tearing this thing up at night now and I love it. The changes with my husband are subtle, but I am noticing them."

With a naughty look on her face, Rachelle asked, laughing, "Wow, what do you think has caused such a shift in his behavior? Does he watch porn? That does it for some men."

"I really don't know, but I doubt it. That's not really his thing, but I'm not going to complain about anything or question him, for that matter. I'm simply going to keep on enjoying it." She giggled, "And, I am really enjoying it."

"Now, you make me feel like I'm missing out on something."

"What could you possibly be missing out on? You've always said you and George have this wild, crazy, satisfying sex life going on. What more could you want?"

Rachelle laughed, then stopped and looked thoughtful briefly before asking, "Do you think he could be having an affair to account for all these new found skills?"

"Absolutely not," Teyona said, emphatically. "I don't know why you would say such a thing."

"I was only joking. Good grief, can't you take a joke? You know I didn't mean that."

Teyona blew out a puff of air. "I'm sorry, Rachelle. I am just a bit on edge today. Don't pay any attention to me."

"What's going on with you anyway?" Rachelle wanted to know. "You still haven't said."

Teyona was quiet a moment before she said, "I've been having those horrible nightmares again. Had another one last night."

"About Bobby Johnson?"

"Yeah."

"It's been nearly a year since that whole fiasco," Rachelle said, remembering back to the night when Bobby broke into Teyona and Steven's home with

80

the intention of raping her while Steven watched, before killing them both.

Massages completed, Teyona and Rachelle moved into the area to have their nails done. Once seated, they sunk their feet into the foot spa to soak while their manicurists took care of their hands.

Rachelle resumed their conversation, "Do you think that's it?" she asked.

"It's hard to say but it's possible. It will be a year in two weeks."

"That has to be unsettling for you to have those terrible memories brought back up again. The nightmares could be recurring because it is approaching the anniversary?"

"That could very well be. I think it's either that or because of the guy that I saw that night at the art show who looked so much like Bobby."

"Talk to me about the nightmares. Are they always the same?"

"Yes, they are always the same. He's always raping me."

"Raping you or trying to rape you?"

"Rachelle, will you pay attention, please. I said in the nightmares, he is always raping me, brutally."

Rachelle snapped her head in either directions and said, "My goodness, where are the cameras?"

With a confused expression on her face, Teyona asked, "What are you talking about?"

"I thought you were auditioning for the Real Housewives of Columbia."

"What?"

"You were being so dramatic," Rachelle said and illustrated with her hands adding, "Pay attention, please."

"Do you take anything serious? This is not funny. Do you think I'm kidding around with this? Well, I'm not. These nightmares are driving me insane and I can't share what I'm experiencing with Steven for obvious reasons."

"I can certainly understand that."

"The thing that concerns me most is that it all seemed so real. It is like Bobby is right there in the house with us. I can't explain it but seriously, it's like I sense him there."

"I don't understand."

"I know. It's odd. Even though I know he's been dead almost a year and that he's never coming back, but it's like he's there in the room, in the bed, watching, menacing."

Rachelle looked thoughtful a moment. "I can see why you would feel that way. That's probably true because of all you went through. That was a horrific situation. That Bobby Johnson was some piece of work. I mean if he were still alive, I would tell you to bolt all your windows and doors and get the best security system that money can buy. Perhaps what happened to him might have been the best possible scenario because it would have been almost impossible to keep him out of your house if he really wanted to get in."

"That's a terrible thing to say."

"But I'm right, aren't I?"

Teyona sighed. "I know."

"It is unfortunate that you don't feel comfortable discussing the nightmares with Steven. It could help."

"There's no way that I could do that. I can't have Steven revisit that situation. It's taking him long enough to put the past behind us, that is if he really has."

"You don't think he has forgiven you and moved past you and Bobby Johnson's saga?"

"I'm not sure. But, if he hasn't, how can I expect him to forgive me when I can't forgive myself?" Teyona said, reached into her purse, pulled from it a pack of cigarettes and a gold lighter. She took a cigarette from the pack and stuck it between her lips.

With a wrinkle in her brow, Rachelle stared at her friend. "When did you start smoking?" she inquired.

"Almost a year," Teyona lit the cigarette and blew out a cloud of smoke away from Rachelle. "I don't do it often. Just when my nerves get the best of me."

Rachelle continued to stare at Teyona.

"What is it?" Teyona asked.

"We've never talked in depth about this but I was just wondering whether you ever thought about Bobby, about what happened between the two of you, you know, before it went crazy there at the end? What you two shared was pretty intense there for a while. Do you ever miss running off in the middle of the night to be with him, what it was like to be with the man who just did it for you?"

Teyona studied the cigarette she held between two fingers, watched it burned away some before she snuffed it out in the crystal ashtray on the table between them. "Not him so much as I think about the situation itself. I mean for heaven's sake I killed a man, I can never forget that."

"Is that it?"

"Rachelle, I killed my lover. Isn't that enough to think about? I just wish I had never come in contact with a Bobby Johnson."

"But you did."

"What is it with you? You are supposed to be my friend but often times, it appears that you are the judge, the jury and the executioner when it comes to me. What do you have against me?"

Rachelle looked at Teyona for what seemed a long time before she replied. "Listen to me, Tee, I don't mean to appear harsh with you or condemn you. I'm really just trying to help you to get through this dilemma. That man was in your home and he was there for one reason. Bobby Johnson intended to kill you and your husband. It was gonna be him or you and Steven, and you did what you had to do. You had no choice!" Rachelle looked her friend squarely in the eyes and said, "What you did was necessary, what you had to do to stop him from harming you and your family. You took his ass out! Self defense! Plain and simple!"

Teyona sighed. "I know but it doesn't make me feel any better knowing that I killed a man and I blame myself totally because I made the choice to," she enumerated with her fingers, "number one, step outside my marriage to a wonderful man, a man who loves me unconditionally and number two, I got involved with someone who was closer to my son's age then mine. Three, I shouldn't have gotten involved with him no matter his age, but the fact that he was a young, crazy as hell, foul talking cuss should have made the situation even less desirable. All I can say is that I will never forget what I did or forgive myself for the position I put my family and myself in."

"It's not easy; I know that but don't beat yourself up too much. When you start to come down on yourself, keep in mind, Tee that if you hadn't done what you did, it would not have ended well for you and Steven. So, just let it go. It was self defense and nothing can change that now."

Teyona signed deeply. "You're right."

"Hell yeah, I'm right. I'm always right."

After a while, Teyona said, "I've noticed some changes in Steven's behavior. There are some things going on with him that concerns me also."

"Didn't you just tell me that things couldn't be better between you two?"

"Our sex life is great. That couldn't be better."

"Then what is it?" Rachelle pressed. "Specifics, please!"

"He's changing in ways that I can't quite wrap my mind around."

"Like?" Rachelle appeared annoyed.

"He drinks more than usual which is not like Steven. You know how he feels about alcohol. Usually he would have one drink or two but never before had he ever pulled out a bottle and a glass and brings the whole bottle into the den or even up to bed. And, get this, most nights before he comes home now, he stops off at Jimmy's and have a couple of drinks."

"Jimmy's?"

"Yes, almost every night. Something else odd about his current behavior, I catch him staring at me but when I ask him why he's doing it, he denies it. I feel he's doing it a lot more when he thinks I'm not paying attention. That alarms me sometimes."

"You are not afraid of him, are you?" Rachelle asked in surprise, leaning closer to Teyona.

"No, Steven would never hurt me. He loves me too much but sometimes I think he still questions how I could hurt him as I did."

Rachelle shook her head and took a sip of her champagne. "I haven't noticed anything. He seems the same to me."

"Are you sure? You have such insight into people and you and Steven are so close." Teyona sighed. "I don't have a problem figuring out other people's lives and working with them to get them on the right path, but when it comes to my own life, I'm completely at a loss," Teyona stated and taking a sip from her glass. "And you are sure you haven't noticed anything different about him?"

"No, I haven't," Rachelle said and smiled, "I really don't think you have anything to worry about where Steven is concerned but just leave the man alone. As long as he treats you well and continues to handle that ass correctly, you should let the rest of this bull shit go. I do hope you get a fix on the Bobby Johnson's situation though. That negro is dead. Let him stay there, okay."

"Gee, you think."

Then Rachelle said, "So Dr. Steve is hung like a bull, huh?"

"Seriously." Teyona gave her friend a look. "Girl, stop."

Rachelle chuckled and said, "Well?" looking over her wineglass.

Teyona and Rachelle giggled and.

"Who would ever think I'm a therapist listening to the conversation we're having," Teyona said and they chuckled.

"I don't know what you're talking about. Hell, even the most conservative women want a man with a big dick who knows how to whip that shit around."

Teyona and Rachelle laughed so hard that the manicurists joined in.

"You're so stupid," Teyona said, they laughed some more and sipped champagne.

"It is what it is," Rachelle lifted a hand in a nonchalant gesture.

A sudden thought sprouted in Teyona's mind. "Speaking of men with big dicks and know how to whip them around, Steven said once if we weren't married that he'd date you."

Champagne shot out of Rachelle's mouth. "What," she exclaimed, using the back of her hand to brush away the liquid that had fallen from her mouth onto her chin.

"That's right. We were just having a simple conversation one night. Talking about things we did in high school, college, people we knew in the past, and people we would date if we weren't married and your name came up."

"I don't believe this shit."

"It's true." Teyona gave a tiny shrug and took another small sip from her glass. "Steven said had he not met and married me, he would've asked you out."

"I think that is just so weird." She shook her head slowly, staring off toward the far side of the room.

"No it's not. Rachelle, you are a gorgeous woman and if Steven and I weren't in a relationship and you two were in the same town and unattached, I can see him dating you. What's weird about that?"

"Well weird might not be the right word but I just can't imagine that."

"Considering where we are right now, I can't either," Teyona said and they laughed.

"You've got yourself a great man there, girl," Rachelle said wistfully.

"I know," Teyona breathed.

Once dressed, they left the spa. Outside in the warm night air, walking towards their cars, Teyona said, "I'll call you tomorrow."

"Alright," Rachelle said, a troubled expression on her face.

"Are you okay? Is something bothering you?" Teyona paused at Rachelle's car, noticing the sudden change in her friend's behavior.

Rachelle was thinking she'd rather go anywhere but home, but she said, "I used to know George so well but I don't have any idea what going on in his mind lately." Teyona took a closer look at Rachelle as she continued. "When we talk, we argue, he is behaving very irresponsibly, childish. Six months ago, he quit his job at Daktar Marketing. He'd worked there for fifteen years and he worked his way up to Vice President. He's telling me that he and a couple of guys are starting their own business. Since that time, I don't know what the hell he's doing. Seems to me that all he does is hang out in bars half the night, and mopes around the house during the day. That's all I see and the last couple of months, it's become even worst. He always seemed depressed, he doesn't go out with me or spend time with our friends and he seldom engages in conversation with me and you know how I love to talk."

"George has been talking about going into business for himself for a while now. I thought that was in the works and is the reason that we don't get together as much lately."

"Well, I'm not seeing any progress in that department and he's not saying a damn thing to me."

"Rachelle, why haven't you said anything? Here I am dumping my worries on you when you have issues of your own. I am so sorry. I had no idea that you and George were having issues. What are you going to do about you and George? Have you and George thought about getting some counseling?"

"We haven't talked about it. As I said, we seldom talk."

"Don't let this situation get too far out of hand. Stop what you're doing for a second, take a good look at your marriage and do what you need to do to get it back on track. You don't want to let something like this go on too long. Handle it now."

"We'll see."

"Promise me you two will get some help if you need to."

"Don't worry about us, girl. It is what it is."

"No, promise me, Rachelle. You're married to a great guy. You don't want to lose that."

"I hear ya," Rachelle dragged out but thinking, she was the prize in that marriage. Not George!

"Get home safely."

"You too."

The two women embraced, got into their cars with Rachelle saying under her breath, "I wish I had a man like Steven to go home to." Then, she drove away from the spa.

CHAPTER 9

RACHELLE

Rachelle drove through the gate where she lived in a very affluent community and drove up the beautiful tree lined driveway before shutting off the engine. She entered her beautifully furnished, four bedroom home through the front door and from the foyer, she saw George sitting on the couch in the den, staring at the TV that was playing loudly. She walked over to him and snatched the remote from his hand. "Why do you have the volume up so loud?" she asked, turning down the volume before tossing the remote on the couch.

"How are you too, wifey?" George replied, wondering about the change in his wife's attitude. He had tried talking to her, tried sharing his career choices with her but nothing he did interested her or seemed to please her. She had shut him down so often that he had started keeping quiet about what was going on in his career, his life. How long could a man endure his woman, his wife discounting everything he had to say, and the things he was trying to do—in short discount him. Enough was enough! George had recently decided that he'd go on with his business plans and if Rachelle chose to be involved, then he'd be pleased, but if she wasn't with him one hundred percent as he'd always been with her about her endeavors, then he would just not waste anymore time trying to convince her to come on board.

Rachelle gave him an evil look. "I hope you haven't been sitting on that couch all day. Did you even go out and looked for work today?"

"I just walked through the door five minutes ago, Rachelle," George answered his wife, looking at her with a confused look on his handsome face. "And why would I go out looking for work when you know that Geoff, Marcus and I will be opening our marketing firm in a couple of weeks? I've been trying to tell you about this for almost a year. Where have you been?" George was ecstatic that he'd resigned from his Vice Presidency at Daktar Marketing months ago because he and two of his friends were going into business together but was annoyed that Rachelle was acting as if she didn't have a clue about what was going on. Her nonchalant attitude about anything that interested him was the reason he'd chosen to talk as little about his work as possible with her. Rachelle loved progress at its ending stages. She wasn't much for the process. It appeared the more successful her friends became, the angrier she became with him which made no sense.

"You mentioned you were going into business for yourself but I haven't seen any progress and you seem to keep everything bottled up inside. What am I suppose to do smell what's going on inside your damn mind?"

"Forget about it, Rachelle," George said, leaping up from the couch, giving up on trying to reach any part of Rachelle that she didn't want to be reached. "I'm going to bed."

Rachelle stared at his receding back as he headed toward the stairs. She took in a deep breath, dropped her purse and keys on the table and checked the time on her watch. It was almost nine thirty that evening. She had no intention of going to bed now, having had another disagreement with George or sit around the house alone. She was going to enjoy herself. She worked hard and tonight she intended to party even harder.

She went upstairs, pinning her hair up atop of her head, took a shower, and after smoothing some of her favorite scented lotion over her body, she then squeezed into a little red dress that revealed a good amount of cleavage and showed off the curves of her hot body. She slipped into a pair of black strappy four inch heels and after accessorizing with pieces of gold jewelry, she grabbed a black purse and within the hour, she was backing out of her driveway. Twenty minutes later, she pulled her car into one of the few available parking spaces at Jimmy's Bar & Grill, and entered the semi-crowded, dimly lit room. Rachelle turned heads as she moved deeper inside the bar, craning her neck as she scanned the room in the hope of seeing a familiar face, one in particular. People were mingling, enjoying lively conversations, others were dancing while waitresses milled around, serving drinks to patrons as cigarette smoke and the sounds of loud old school music floated in the atmosphere.

Disappointed upon not seeing anyone she knew, she inwardly sighed, walked over to sit on an available stool at the bar and began bobbing her head to the upbeat music emitting from a large speakers on the walls in the bar.

The bartender approached, wiped down the counter in front of her and pleasantly asked, "What can I get for you this evening?"

She greeted him with a pleasant smile of her own and replied, "I'll have a Mimosa, please."

"Coming right up," the bartender said. He walked away and returned quickly to place a napkin and Rachelle's drink in front of her.

She lifted her purse from her shoulder and removed several bills from her wallet to pay for her drink when she felt a light tap on her shoulder. She turned to see who it was and was pleasantly surprised. "Oh, Steven, hi," she greeted, feeling a bit of a ripple jet through her body.

She was about to place some bills on the counter for her drink when Steven held up his hand to stop her. "I've got this," he said, opening his wallet, taking out a few bills and throwing them on the bar.

"Thank you," she said returning the bills to her wallet.

With his hands on her shoulders, Steven kissed Rachelle on her cheek. "You're looking fantastic tonight," he said checking out the dress that had risen halfway up her thighs.

"You always clean up well, yourself." She complimented him in return and turning a sly eye to him said, "But you know that, don't you?"

He smiled, taking the stool next to her. "What are you doing here tonight?" he asked. The bartender returned, picked up the bills, wiped down the counter and looked questioningly at Steven. "Scotch on the rocks, please," he answered the look.

"I just thought I'd come out and get a drink before going home and going to bed," she replied, not sharing with Steven her real reason for being there. She'd hope that he'd be there.

Steven teasingly shook a finger in her direction, "Right, when you've got a perfectly well stocked bar in your home. You've got to do better than that. Besides, I know you. You wouldn't be out here alone unless you had something heavy on your mind. Are things alright with you and George?" Rachelle looked at Steven and suddenly burst into tears. Surprised, he slid closer to her and placed his arm around her shoulders. "What's going on? You and George are having some issues? Come on," he urged her, "you know you can talk to me."

"He doesn't talk to me, we're arguing all the time, he's not working, and spending all our money on who knows what. Everything is all messed up. I sometimes think he's having an affair and I don't know what to do about it," she said, removing tissues from her purse to wipe away tears from her eyes.

Steven had no way of knowing that Rachelle wasn't telling him the whole truth and her crocodile tears were only for his benefit. "Who? George? George isn't having an affair," he smiled dubiously, shaking his head negatively. "Look, don't cry. I'm sure you two will work things out. All couples go through ups and downs, that little rough patch, but George is a good man, he loves you, and you love him so I'm sure you two will work it all out."

"I'm not sure I love him anymore, Steven. Sometimes, he's just not a very nice man."

"Ahh, come on. George is one of the nicest guys that I know," Steven declared.

"If you say so." She looked skeptically at him.

"What does that mean?"

"He's changed, Steven. He doesn't have that drive he once had."

"I don't believe that for a minute. Aren't George and a couple of friends in the process of launching their business soon? I talked with him about a month or so ago and it seems he's been putting in a lot of work for the opening. That's what he told me. He's wanted to start his own company for a while now, right? When someone is starting a business, it takes a lot of hard work and an enormous amount of time, so if George has been missing in action, you know it's not on purpose. The man is working, Ma."

"I really don't know what that man is doing. Lately, there seems to be a serious disconnect between us and I don't know where that's coming from or how to handle it."

96

Steven gave Rachelle's shoulder a squeeze before he released her and sat up straight on his stool. He lifted his drink glass to Rachelle and said, "It's all gonna work out. You'll see. Here's to an amazing evening at home with our spouses."

Rachelle glanced up at him. She shrugged, rolled her eyes as she and Steven clicked their glasses together, and said, "Whatever."

Steven shook his head and grinned.

"I congratulated your wife earlier on your recent honor and I want to congratulate you as well. That cover shot on the magazine is gorgeous. We should go out and celebrate, that is if I can get George to cooperate."

"George will be fine."

Rachelle cleared her throat. She couldn't help the sly smile that touched her lips when one of her favorite songs began to play, she said, "Screw it." She leaped from the stool. "I wanna dance. Come dance with me." She extended her hands to Steven.

He took a huge swallow from his drink, got up from his stool and taking her hand in his, led her to the small dance floor, with Rachelle thinking she couldn't have better scripted the way the evening was going.

On the dance floor, Rachelle moved into Steven's arms, the seductive fragrance of her perfume sent a powerful shudder through him. He closed his eyes and their bodies melted together in perfect sync as they moved to the music that filled the bar. She bit back a moan and said, wistfully, "I wish George was more like you, Steven."

Steven looked down at her and smiled. At that moment, she thought he was the sexiest man alive. "There's nothing wrong with George, woman. This is just a little bump in the road, a temporary setback. In the next day or two, you are gonna be completely in love with your man again so I'm not putting any stock into what you are saying right now, okay," he said, smiling down at Rachelle. She responded by reaching up, taking his face in both hands and briefly kissing him on the tip of his nose. Pulling away from him, for an instant their eyes locked. After a moment, he looked away but wrapped both arms around her, holding her a little tighter with her clinging to him, her head resting on his chest as they continued dancing.

The next song filling the room was a club favorite, causing a stir in the bar and the dance floor became crowded.

"I forgot what a terrific dancer you are," Rachelle said to Steven.

"You are quite the dancer yourself," he acknowledged. Dancing apart, Rachelle pulled out her most provocative dance moves; twisting her body from side to side in a hot, sensuous display of her dance talents, snapping her raised fingers in the air, turning her back to him, grinding deep into his crouch. He tactfully moved away from her gyrating buttock only a second before she was pressed against him again.

Once the song was over, Steven looked at his watch and said, "I'd better be getting home. I've got some early morning appointments. What about

you? You gonna hang out here for a while or can I
see you to your car?"

"No, I guess I'll head out as well," she replied.
"And, yes, you may see me to my car."

Steven and Rachelle left the bar together;
walking her to her car, he held the door open for her
and gave her a quick kiss on the cheek. As he turned
to walk away, she caught his hand, pulling him back
to her. She parted her legs, guided his hand under
her dress to her bare feminine treasure and held it
there until he laughed and pulled away.

He stood up straight, closed the door to her car
and said, "Get home safely, Rachelle."

"You're no fun tonight, Steven," she said
through pouty lips.

"What can I say?" He walked toward his car and
waved to her as she sped by him, leaving the
parking lot.

CHAPTER 10

STEVEN & TEYONA

Steven entered his house to see Teyona sitting at the kitchen table with papers scattered around on it. She was busy writing on a legal pad. She looked up. "Hey babe," she greeted.

"Hey." He removed his coat, hung it across the back of a chair and kissed his wife before he took a seat at the table.

"Can I get you anything?"

"No, I'm just gonna take a drink up to bed."

"Are you sure? I made one of your favorite roasts."

"You did? Ahhh, that sounds really great. Perhaps I'll have some tomorrow night." He yawned and stretched.

"Okay."

"What's going on here?" he asked referencing all the papers on the table yawning again.

"I'm giving a presentation to a group of social studies graduate students tomorrow and I'm organizing a few notes."

"Looks like you've been busy, that's a lot of work. I hope you're not gonna be up all night."

"It won't be long now. I'm just about finished."

"You'll never guess who I ran into at Jimmy's tonight."

With wide eyed anticipation, Teyona said, glancing up at him. "I have no idea. Who?"

"Rachelle."

"Rachelle? Was George with her?"

"No, he wasn't," he answered and asked, "What's going on with them anyway?"

"Why, what did she say?" she asked and added, grinning, "I'll bet she was hanging all over you all night as usual."

Letting that remark slide, Steven said, "She was having a moment where she was just not that into George but I assured her that in a day or two, she'll be more in love with him than ever."

"You know her so well."

"She congratulated us and suggested we go out to celebrate our accomplishments."

"That would be great," Teyona said. Since they had opened offices in three other cities, it'd been several months since she and her husband had gone out on a date night, especially with another couple and she'd already begun to look forward to it. "It would be nice to get together with Rachelle and George and hopefully we can figure out what's going on with the two of them."

101

"They're gonna be just fine."

"I hope so," she looked up at him with a serious expression on her face. "They're our friends and I want them to be okay. If something is wrong and if we can help, I'd like us to try." She laid her pen on the table and said "There, all done."

Steven reached across the table and touched his wife's hand. They gazed into each other's eyes. She got up, walked around the table, stood behind him, and begun to massage his shoulders.

"Ummm." He moved his neck from side to side, removing the kinks.

"Feels good?"

"Feels great." His eyes closed, she could feel her husband's body relaxing.

After about ten minutes, she said, "Okay, don't go to sleep down here. Go on up. I'll be up in a few minutes." She went back around the table to her seat.

He got up and after picking up his jacket from the chair, went over to the cabinet, took out a bottle of scotch from one of the shelves and a glass from the counter. "I'll see you upstairs," he said and was about to leave the kitchen.

Teyona frowned, noticing the bottle of Scotch that Steven was about to take upstairs again. "Steven."

He turned and looked at her. "Yeah."

"Are we okay?" she couldn't stop herself from asking.

Steven blinked at her. "Yeah, we're fine." He loved his wife, he loved her very much but had he betrayed her in the worst way? Yes, he had. Almost a year ago, Teyona had cheated on him but long before her affair with Bobby Johnson, he'd had several affairs, but would he allow her to find out about them and possibly end his marriage? No way. "Why did you ask that?"

"In the past several months it seems you're drinking a little more than before."

"Really?"

"Of course you are."

Steven smiled. "I love you, if that answers your question. I will always love you and nothing will ever change that."

Teyona put her pencil down and looked thoughtfully at Steven, "I know you work hard and I know about your commitment to your patients, but you really don't seem to be yourself and you don't have much time for us anymore. No matter what you were doing, you always had time for us. I know Rachelle suggested an outing for us and I'm happy about that, but....." She paused a moment. Then she said, "But if you say everything is fine, then I'll take you at your word."

Steven pulled out his chair again and sat. "Yes baby. Things are fine with us. Things are great." Then, he added, "Look, you are right, we haven't spent very much time together lately, but I'll tell you what. Why don't we set up something with Rachelle and George soon and go out for a night of fun for a change? We haven't done that in a while or if you want, I'll come home early tomorrow. You and I could go out to dinner and later, get our dance on." He rose from the chair and did a little dance. "How does that sound? We'll make it a date night."

Teyona smiled up at Steven, thinking she'd never known a more caring, supportive man and she loved him more than she could say. "Well?" Steven pressed.

"You really want to?"

"Absolutely."

Teyona smiled. "I'm concerned about Rachelle and George so why don't I give her a call tomorrow and see what we can work out?"

"Sounds good to me."

"Go on up and I'll be up soon," Teyona said and began scooping up her papers into a pile.

"I'll wait for you," he said and instead of taking the bottle of Scotch upstairs, he returned it to the cabinet, placing the glass back on the counter and left the kitchen to go upstairs.

Teyona sat at the table a little while longer. After the tragic situation involving Bobby Johnson, she'd taken seven months off from her practice and didn't return until she felt comfortable enough to be able to help others without it interfering with her own recovery. She'd been back at work the past three months and she was getting new patients almost every week. Additionally, she'd started giving speeches to college students and social workers, imparting valuable information and assistance to them in any way that she could.

After slipping the papers into her briefcase, she shut off the lights and went upstairs. Entering the bedroom, she heard a low rumble coming from

Steven and knew her husband was asleep. She slid out of her robe and eased under the covers nestling against him.

On Friday night, Teyona and Steven drove out to the upscale Infinity Restaurant and Nightclub, near where they lived, meeting Rachelle and George. Because of the food, the legendary nightlife and atmosphere, the restaurant and nightclub was frequented by the well-to-do and well-connected; politicians, college professors and educators, doctors, lawyers, athletes and patrons from neighboring cities and states.

Steven, dressed in a dark blue suit with a pale blue shirt, got out of his car, walked around it and opened the door for Teyona. She was wearing a black pencil skirt that ended mid calf, a white flowing blouse that stopped at her waist in front and fell below the hips in back, and black three inch sling back heels. She carried a matching purse, diamond earrings hung from her ear lobes and a diamond bracelet adorned her wrist.

They entered the elegant restaurant to see Rachelle and George waiting for them. "Hello you two," Teyona greeted them and after a quick embrace, they were ushered through the room with tables draped in white linen table cloths, matching napkin in holders and lit candles. "I can't believe we didn't have to wait for you," Teyona gently nudged Rachelle in the side and gave her a teasing giggle.

"Ah shut up," Rachelle came back and they chuckled, as Steven and George followed them to their table.

The waitress took their dinner orders, George said to her, "Please bring us a bottle of your best champagne after our meal."

"Very good, Sir," the waitress said and left.

"Here, here," Steven said, and the men shared a fist bump as the women chuckled.

"Rachelle, my friend Josie called me earlier and she said Bloomingdale's has some of the best items in stock right now. She even mentioned a couple of high end boutiques that really have some nice things," Teyona said across the table to her friend.

"Are you thinking what I'm thinking?" Rachelle asked, excitedly.

"Yes. New York and Bloomies here we come," Teyona joined in. "Why don't we check our calendars and come up with a time that is convenient for both of us and let's fly out there. We could make it a day trip or we could do an overnighter."

"I'm all about shopping so that sounds like fun."

"Yeah, we are overdue. Give me a call tonight or early in the morning and I will make reservations and call Josie with our plans."

"Speaking of shopping," Rachelle began, "there's a new boutique over on Decker and they've got some really cute little pieces. Give them a look. I think you will find something cute and sexy that you might like."

"I've heard of that store but I haven't been there yet. I'll check them out."

"Looks like the girls are gonna be going on another one of their famous shopping sprees," Steven said to George, shaking his head.

"Looks that way," George growled.

"Next step is filing bankruptcy," Steven grinned.

George's smile was almost a grimace. "Brother, you don't know the half of it," he said and both men roared.

"What are they laughing at," Teyona asked, leaning towards Rachelle.

"Who cares," she replied and she and Teyona chuckled.

Their meal of steaks, lobster, potatoes, asparagus, peas, carrots, salads, bread, water and wine were placed on the table within a reasonable time and as the couples ate they carried on light conversations.

Teyona tried to see if there was anything out of the ordinary in the dynamic between Rachelle and George. Nothing on his part, she thought; however, she did notice that most of Rachelle's conversation was directed to Steven. But what else was new. She had always had a fancy for Steven so it wasn't unusual that the two of them dominated the conversation.

After dinner, a bottle of Dom Perignon was brought to their table. George made the toast after all their glasses were filled. "I just want to congratulate both of you, Teyona and Steven being named the Medical Power Couple of the South.

That's quite a statement and on behalf of my wife, we are so proud of both of you and are extremely happy to call you our friends."

"Yes, congrats," Rachelle said and they clicked their champagne glasses together.

After consuming a couple glasses of champagne, they went into the nightclub and immediately hit the dance floor. They danced to some old school music and remained on the floor as other popular songs flowed from the speakers. The couples danced with each other, exchanged partners, then, the men watched the women clown around on the dance floor together.

After some time, they left the dance floor and returned to their seats, Steven said, "George, I see that you guys are approaching the launch date for your new company."

"Yeah. Little more than a week now. We are excited about it," George said and glanced at Rachelle who gave a small smile but didn't comment.

"That is wonderful, George. It looks like congratulations are in order for you two as well," Teyona said. "I wish you much success."

"Thanks so much. Everything is on schedule. It looks good," George said, happily.

Rachelle still didn't comment.

They danced a little more, had more champagne and an hour later, the couples left the club and drove home.

Teyona asked, "What did you think about Rachelle and George tonight?"

"I thought tonight went well."

"Rachelle didn't have very much to say to George or anything about his business venture."

"Well, they danced together."

"That's about all they did because she didn't engage him in conversation even when he tried. She answered him but nothing else. It wasn't a continuous conversation between them and I noticed several times that George was trying. I have to give him credit for that."

"Nothing stood out for me. I thought we were all having fun."

"You and I were having fun, Steven, but you probably didn't notice that Rachelle wasn't talking to George because she was busy talking to you all night."

"No more than usual," Steven replied and glanced over at Teyona.

"You don't think she's having an affair, do you?"

"Why would you say that?"

"Well, she seems to share a lot with you so I thought it might be more comfortable for her to say something to you if she were because she probably wouldn't think you'd be judgmental."

"I don't know. If she were having an affair, I imagine you'd be the one she'd tell. You're the least judgmental person that I know."

"I'm not sure she would agree," Teyona said and pausing before saying, "I really am concerned about the way she treats him and I think she makes up things about him that aren't true. Who does that?"

"You think so?"

"Yes, I do. I hate to say it but I believe that to be true."

"I think whatever is going on with them will smooth itself out."

"Maybe I should talk with her again," Teyona said, helpfully. "I don't want to get all up in her business without an invitation and if she was anyone else, I wouldn't but she's my best friend and I can't sit around, watch something bad happening and not try to do something to stop it. If she invites me out of her life, I will happily remove myself from their situation." She paused again. "But, there's definitely something going on with my girl."

CHAPTER 11

TEYONA & RACHELLE

Two days later, Teyona and Rachelle settled on a day trip. They boarded United Blue Airlines, flew to New York and were met at LaGaurdia Airport by their friend, Josie. She drove them to Fifth Avenue and the three women stopped off at a coffee shop where they decided over lattes which stores they would shop.

"It is always so great to see you, Josie," Teyona said, smiling over her latte.

"Same here, girl," Josie replied, reaching across the table to touch Teyona's hand. "I've got to make it a point to visit South Carolina more often."

"I know you are in a relatively new position in a new company and it would probably be difficult to get away, but if you can make it happen, that would be great."

"Teyona told me you're in charge of creative activities in this huge advertising agency," Rachelle said.

"Yeah and it is the most exciting job I've ever had. I get to see my ideas in action," Josie, the tall, beautiful, model-like forty-two year old woman, gushed. "It is so rewarding."

"What kind of clients do you get?" Rachelle asked.

"The sky is the limit with us. We don't turn anyone away. We put together campaigns for any entity from model agencies to the auto industry, cereal, cosmetic companies."

"That is terrific, Josie," Teyona said. Five years ago, Josie left a teaching position in Charleston and moved to New York where she was able to take advantage of her Marketing Degree she earned at Columbia University in New York. Her father passed away when she was in her senior year in college and after graduating, she returned to Charleston to assist in caring for her ailing mother who passed away a year later. Six months later, Josie moved back to New York to pursue her career. She met Frank twenty five years ago while in college, they married two years later and had two children; a son and a daughter and two grandchildren. "I'm proud of all you've accomplished in such a short period of time."

"Thank you," Josie accepting the compliment. "I wish you guys were staying at least one night in the city. There's so much to do; greats plays, the club scene, museums, wonderful eating places."

"Teyona is never gonna be away from Steven on a Saturday," Rachelle grinned.

"You and Steven still do the Saturday thing, huh?" Josie chuckled.

"Yeah, girl," Teyona laughed, then asked, "How are Frank, Kaleah and Joshua?"

And Rachelle said, "Forget Frank and the kids, I want to hear all about the grand kids."

That brought chuckles from the women.

"They are all just perfect," Josie removed her wallet from her purse and began showing her friends photos of her grandchildren. "This is Aaliyah and this is Josh, Jr." She handed her wallet to Teyona.

"Ahhh, they're so cute." Teyona took a good look at the pictures before she passed the wallet on to Rachelle.

Rachelle took the wallet and viewed the pictures. "Yes, they are," she agreed.

"Each of my children has satisfied grandma immensely," Josie shared.

The ladies chuckled and sipped lattes in between viewing photos.

Finally, they left the coffee shop and began their day of shopping, hitting as many of the high end stores and boutiques as they could before stopping at an outdoors bistro for lunch. Later, laden with purchases, they bought a couple of large suitcases to pack their purchases in. That Friday evening they said goodbye to Josie and after promising they would return to the city in a month or two, they boarded the plane and returned to South Carolina.

Once in the air, the captain's soothing calm voice came over the intercom, addressing them, "Good evening, ladies and gentlemen, welcome to United Blue Airlines, Flight 289 to Columbia, SC. We will be cruising at twenty-eight thousand feet and should be arriving in Columbia in an hour and fifteen minutes. Keep all seat belts fastened until further notice. Enjoy the flight and thank you for flying with United Blue." A short time later, the seatbelt notification buzzed, informing passengers that seatbelts could be disengaged, Teyona directed her attention away from the window, looked at Rachelle and placed a hand gently on Rachelle's hand. "I'd like to talk to you but first, let me say this. If I am intruding into your privacy and you want me out, just say so."

"What do you want to know," Rachelle replied, politely.

"You remember the conversation we had about you and George and you told me all these negative things about him?"

"Yeah."

"Well, when we were out together the other night, I didn't notice any of it. What's going on with you, woman? Talk to me!"

Rachelle looked pensively. "I think because of the stress of the job and all that's going on that I just get a little ahead of myself and George is my easiest target. I'll either pick on him, ignore him or I'm just not interested in anything he has to say."

"How long has this been going on?"

"Not quite a year."

114

"Do you think it's right to treat your husband this way? Doesn't he deserve better?" Teyona asked, gently.

Rachelle head jerked sharply. "What about me?" She snapped. "Don't I deserve better?"

Teyona eyes grew wide. She was shocked and stunned by Rachelle's outburst. In all the years they'd been friends, she'd never seen this side of Rachelle. She felt somewhat like she was talking with a stranger more than her friend. "What do you mean?" Teyona rolled her eyes. "Rachelle, George treats you like a queen. He adores you, provides for your every need. You don't have to work if you didn't want to. He cooks, he cleans, he even serves you breakfast in bed with a rose. Girl, there aren't many men like George that actually love women and want to be with one. You can't find a better man than George."

It was Rachelle's turn to roll her eyes. She reclined back into her seat. "Yes, George does all that for me but do I have to be satisfied with what I have?" Again, Teyona's eyes went wide. She thought to herself why wouldn't a woman be satisfied with that? Rachelle continued on, "I want more, Teyona. Is it so wrong for me to want more for myself?" She sighed deeply.

"Are you saying you are not satisfied with your husband anymore?" Teyona asked tactfully, a knot in her stomach forming in anticipation to her friend's answer.

Rachelle, still lounging back in her seat with her eyes closed and hands gripping both armrests offered, "No, as a matter of fact I'm not. I haven't been happy with George for some time now."

"I had no idea. I thought you guys would work through your issues," Teyona said, surprised by that revelation. "What are you gonna do?"

"Honestly, I don't know." Rachelle confessed.

"You're not thinking divorce, are you?"

"I said I don't know." Her eyes opened and a small smile crossed her lips, "You are the therapist, why don't you tell me what I should do?"

Teyona ignored Rachelle's attempt at humor. Her friend's marriage was in jeopardy. Both Rachelle and George were good people. She was concerned and wanted things to work out for the best. "Have you thought about talking with someone, a counselor? I'm not suggesting that you talk to me. I know a number of reputable counselors and I can recommend someone if you want." Teyona began searching her purse for her tablet but was stopped by Rachelle's voice.

"Teyona," Rachelle began, the seriousness of her tone, caused Teyona to stop searching her bag and direct her entire attention to Rachelle. "I don't know that I'm interested in saving my marriage. George and I have grown so far apart. We don't have anything in common, absolutely no shared interest, and as you know, life is short. I want to enjoy the rest of mine."

Teyona stuttered momentarily in astonishment before recovering her senses, "Don't make any hasty decisions before you have had an opportunity to speak with someone. Promise me that." Rachelle

116

just looked at Teyona. She took Rachelle's hands in hers. "Promise me, Rachelle."

"I promise I won't make any hasty decisions." Rachelle said with a yawn, closing her eyes and reclining back into her seat.

CHAPTER 12

RUSSELL

That evening, Russell drove to the building where Steven worked. Russell had been in town more than a month now and he'd become familiar with all the players involved in the death of his brother along with some who may not have been. He'd come to know their habits: their likes, dislikes, where they worked, ate, hung out, who their friends were and who they were sleeping with. Over the past three weeks, he'd been keeping watch at the medical office building and until tonight, he had seen nothing out of the ordinary.

He lit a cigarette and pulled deeply on it. A short time later, Russell grounded out a cigarette before checking his watch. It was eleven forty-five. He lit up another cigarette. He didn't smoke often, only when things weren't working out as he hoped. Just as he was about to start up his car, through the haze of smoke he blew out, he saw several people leave the building. The parking lot was well-lit and Russell clearly saw Dr. Steven Carter and he wasn't alone. Russell's antenna turned up and he quickly extinguished his third cigarette. "Well, well, well," Russell said, as he watched Dr. Carter interacting with his pretty companion. "What's going on with the good doctor? I wonder what he has on tap tonight!" Russell said as he hunched over the steering wheel of his car. He lifted his camera from the passenger seat and after focusing, he began snapping pictures. He'd been observing the doctor for several weeks and initially, he thought the doctor was simply a conscientious fellow, wanting the best for his patients, a loving husband and great family man. By his observation of the man, he appeared damn near perfect. Russell couldn't help but wonder whether anyone could be that good. And though he hated the man, Russell had found himself beginning to respect him somewhat and he felt he should focus his attention on other members of that party. Yet his vow of vengeance for his brother's death wouldn't let him ignore Dr. Carter so he decided to keep his investigations going a few more days.

Dr. Steven Carter walked with a woman out to her car and they spoke briefly before he returned to his office. From Russell's vantage point in the parking lot, he couldn't hear what they were saying nor could they see him since his car was partially obstructed by shrubbery.

Russell removed a small flashlight from the glove compartment, opened the folder on the passenger seat and waived the small light across several pictures. "Ahh," he said, studying the faces in the pictures before shutting off the flashlight and returning the pictures to the folder. With his camera and phone in hand, he got out of his car, making his way across the parking lot, snaking between the buildings in route to the only office that still had its lights on.

There were shards of light escaping the window through the blinds that were slightly opened. Russell inched up close to the window and peered though the blinds. What he saw was much more of a surprise to him than fun to watch. Dr. Carter was sitting on the foot of one of the patient's beds in one of the examining room with his pants around his feet and a woman with blond hair was on her knees with the good doctor's penis in her mouth. The way she masterfully moved her mouth around the head on the man's erect penis caused Russell to experience an involuntary erection of his own. So the good doctor wasn't as squeaky clean as he wanted everyone to believe, Russell thought.

Since the opening in the blinds was small, Russell pulled his phone from his pocket, set it on video and pressed record to document what was happening before his eyes. Done servicing his manly parts, the woman rose to her feet and lifted her skirt to offer herself to the doctor, but he stopped her. He checked his watch, climbed down from the table and pulled up his pants. Whatever the doctor said to the pretty young nurse wasn't what she wanted to hear according to the way she was

120

pouting. Abby had to admit that as special and wonderful as she'd thought their first night in the office together had been, it apparently hadn't been the same for Steven. Had he used her, she wondered, but when he took her into his arms and kissed her thoroughly, hungrily, all her previous doubts drifted away. Dr. Carter gently patted her on her behind, grabbed his coat from the hook behind the door and they left the office; her through the side door, him through the front.

Though satisfied with what he'd discovered that night, Russell still wasn't finished with the good doctor. He felt there was much left to be known. If the doctor had been able to keep this side secret from Russell all this time, he was certain the doctor had much more going on than anyone would've ever think. Russell returned to his car and drove to the hotel. There was no reason to follow the doctor further that night.

Russell decided to return to Dr. Steven Carter's office two nights later to see if there was anything else he could find out before he made a visit to the doctor's wife. At ten o'clock that evening, he rolled into the parking lot across from the medical building and parked. He noticed that there was only one car in the adjourning parking lot. Russell switched off the engine, unhooked his seatbelt and settling comfortably in his seat and lit his first cigarette. He'd only taken two drags when a dark, late model Lexus pulled up, parked next to the doctor's car and the same gorgeous black woman who Russell had witnessed visiting Dr. Carter two nights ago, someone Russell had come to know, emerged from the car. She paused at her car, took out a compact, brushed on some blush and applied some lipstick before making a beeline straight to Dr. Carter's office. Russell wasn't the least bit surprised when the door opened to Dr. Carter's office and she was warmly greeted by the good doctor himself.

Ironically, when the lights at the entry door were turned off, the only room lit was the same room where Russell had spied on the doctor and his nurse two nights before. If the doctor was up to no good again, Russell only hoped his luck would hold out and he'd be able to get another good shot. He eagerly and silently eased out of his car with his camera and phone making his way between the two buildings again and on to the lit window of the office. As he peered in, he saw the doctor and the woman kissing while ripping off each other's clothes.

Russell saw and his phone recorded Dr. Carter unbutton the woman's blouse, slide it down her arms and cast it aside. He reached around, unzipped her skirt letting the fabric fall around her feet, all the while she was busy removing his shirt and helping him out of his pants. In the next instance, they were completely naked and Dr. Carter went to work on the woman's breasts. Capturing a nipple in his mouth and teasing it, feeling it swell and began to stand erect under the assault of his tongue. He moved to the other nipple then the whole breast was in his mouth and his tongue and teeth began their

122

little dance, sending spasms through her body that were unlike anything she'd ever experienced. Then, he enclosed his mouth on her and began to suck hard, causing her to whimper and thrash her body wildly. The woman stroked his penis with expert hands and Russell could tell that she had had her hands on a penis or two in her time.

In one quick movement, Dr. Carter lifted the woman from her feet and on to the bed. The next moment, he was on top of her. He aimed his male hardness into her wet and ready cavity, shoving himself hard into her. She cried out, "Ahhhhhhh." Then, he was plunging wildly into her with her pleading, "Please, Steven, please give it to me. Give it all to me. Please don't stop. Don't ever stop."

Dr. Carter continued to plunge into her. With each skillful stroke, he moved harder into her, faster, he dove deeper with her body responding, meeting his with undeniable fierceness. Russell continued to watch and record their unbridled mating. Although, their actions were extremely passionate, Russell didn't get the sense that there was anything tender or loving about the exchange between them. He got the feeling that the doctor intended to satisfy his partner far more than he was interested in receiving satisfaction himself. The good doctor with the amazing bedside manner was getting his sexual fill right there in his office and his wife had absolutely nothing to do with it.

Russell turned away from the window and walked back to his car. He didn't need to wait to know how the act would end but he did know the doctor was engaging in sexual activities with someone he recognized. Why hadn't she told him she was fucking the good doctor? He wondered.

"Another late night," Teyona said when Steven entered the bedroom where she was sitting up in bed reading.

"I was at the club."

"How did it go? Any of the regulars were there?"

Steven laughed. "It didn't go so well for me but now George was there and he took home a killing."

"So George got lucky tonight, huh? Just gives Rachelle a little more money to spend," Teyona said and they laughed together.

"Yeah. He was on fire, left with a pocket full of money and a huge smile on his face," Steven lied as he walked over to the bed, kissed his wife and began removing his clothes. Shortly afterwards, Teyona heard the shower going in the bathroom.

CHAPTER 13

TEYONA

About two weeks later on a Thursday afternoon,
Teyona was leaving a sporting goods shop where
she'd just purchased a set of golf clubs as a birthday
gift for Steven, when she ran into George.

"George," she said.

"Teyona, how are you?" he greeted her happily
and joked with her saying, "Are these for me?"

They chuckled together.

"This is one of Steven's birthday gifts. His
birthday is not until November but I wanted to get
this gift out of the way. He's been talking about
getting another good set of clubs for over a year
now but he's been so busy running to check on the
other offices that he just hasn't had the time,"
Teyona replied. "And remember, George, you can't
tell him that I already have these for him."

"Mums the word," George said using his hand to
gesture zipping his mouth shut. "That's a really nice

set of clubs." He took the clubs from her hand and examined one of them.

"How is Steven?" He step away from her, motioning a golf swing as he continued, "I haven't seen him in a minute. We should get together again for dinner soon."

Teyona looked at him in surprise. "Weren't you playing with the guys at the club recently?" she asked, recalling her conversation with Steven after he came home late a few nights ago, telling her he'd spent time at the club with George and some of the guys. "Steven said you were there and that you'd won quite a bit of money."

George stopped in mid swing to face Teyona. He shook his head, "No, not me. That must have been one of the other guys. Since we've been putting in so much work before the opening of our new business, I haven't been at the club in a couple of months and now that it is in full swing, I don't know when I'll be able to join the guys for a good game." George paused and grinned. "On top of everything else, I've been taking care of some things around the house. You know your friend. Rachelle always has her famous 'honey do' list and that woman enforces it every chance she get," he said laughing. She joined in but nothing George said was funny especially when he said he'd not played golf with Steven at the club lately after Steven had told her the exact opposite. Why had Steven lied to her? She wondered.

Teyona arrived home, picked up the mail their housekeeper who came in once a week left on the table in the foyer. She dropped her purse, keys and mail on the coffee table, plopped down onto the couch, and began opening the mail. A large manila folder with no return address caught her eye. She opened it and began drawing out the contents of the envelope. Her eyes flew wide open and her hands went over her mouth as the contents fell into her lap. They were pictures of Bobby Johnson! And her! The nightmares had returned, they were back, but who was bringing this madness into her life... again?

Teyona's hands trembled as she looked at the pictures. She felt they were threatening and bewildering at the same time. For Bobby was standing at the front door of the house her and Steven currently resided in. Shaking her head she stared at the pictures some more. This couldn't be real. Bobby was dead. He'd been dead before she and Steven moved into their new home. There was no way he could have known they would buy this house. How could this be? Another picture was of her and Bobby Johnson sitting beside each other on a park bench, and another of them entering a hotel together. She continued to shake her head in disbelief. "No, this can't be right. This, this, is all a lie," she whispered to herself as if to tell herself that it can't be true. But could it be true? As a married woman, she'd done some things with Bobby Johnson that no married woman in her right mind would have done but they'd never gone to a park together and although they'd met often in hotels around town, they'd never gone into one together.

The picture that had stunned and frightened her most was the one of Bobby sitting on her bed in this house with a note attached that read, '*Did you think one bullet could stop me? Did you think you can get rid of me that easy? I can get to you anytime I want to and I really want to. But you already know that, don't you? I still love you. Until we meet again.*'

Teyona became frantic. She ripped the pictures to shreds, tossed the torn pieces into the fireplace and burned them. She rushed upstairs to her bedroom, swiftly crossing the room to her closet where she pulled down the box from the shelf. She carried the box over, laid it on her bed and with shaking hands, she opened the box removing the gun. After staring at the gun intently, she loaded it and slid it under her pillow. She didn't have any idea who was doing this to her but she wasn't going to take any chances. Irene had died in a sanitarium almost a year ago and Bobby Johnson was dead and couldn't come after her, then who was this evil person out there terrifying her? What did this person hope to accomplish? If it was to scare her, then mission accomplished. Those alarming pictures scared the hell out of her.

CHAPTER 14

TEYONA, RACHELLE & RUSSELL

That Saturday morning, Teyona and Rachelle met at their favorite meet up place—the spa. Draped in plush white robes, sitting in expensive deep chairs with a glass of champagne in their hands following deep tissue massages, they relaxed while their feet were being pampered.

Rachelle glanced over at her. "I was surprised to get that call from you this morning," she said, knowing Teyona and Steven usually spend Saturdays together. They'd been spending their Saturdays together since before they were married, that hadn't changed. "This must be serious."

"I'm sorry to disrupt your time with George as well but I have to talk with you."

"Sure, no problem," Rachelle said, taking a sip of champagne. "What's going on?" Noticing the dark circles under Teyona's eyes, she added, "You look tired. Are you alright or are you working too hard as usual? You know you are a workaholic."

"I had a dream about Bobby Johnson again last night," Teyona cut to the chase. "It was more a nightmare than a dream. It seemed so real; he was in my bed again, forcing himself on me."

Rachelle chuckled, "Was it a good wet dream?" She cut her laughter short upon noticing the angry look on Teyona's face and she asked, "Are you alright? You know I was only joking. Tee, we've had this conversation. We know Bobby Johnson is dead and buried. He can't hurt you. Don't let yourself become so bothered by those stupid, senseless dreams or nightmares as you call them."

"That's the least of what is going on with me."

"Details." Rachelle pressed, looking over her glass at Teyona for more information even as she took another sip of champagne.

Teyona took a deep breath, looked around conspiratorially and lowering her voice she said, "Someone is sending me pictures."

"Pictures?" Rachelle gasped excitedly, "Am I supposed to know what that means? Girl, you got to give me the details!"

Before meeting with Rachelle, Teyona did a mental check of the clients she'd seen since going back to work. Noting that there wasn't anything out of the ordinary that would cause anyone to want to come after her, in fact, most of her clients were social workers with work related issues. She even wondered whether Irene really did have a sister who looked like Teyona and was here to cause problems for her. Who really knew what went on inside

Irene's distorted mind? She didn't like someone playing games with her mind, her life.

"Yes, pictures," she answered Rachelle, "pictures of Bobby Johnson and I in places we had never been together."

"You and Bobby Johnson were pretty crazy there for a while, fucking like rabbits, behaving like sex starved kids."

"Don't remind me, only we never did those things that are reflected in the pictures. The pictures I got over a year ago were actual pictures Irene took or had someone take of us when we were together but these pictures can't be real. I can only conclude these pictures are designed to blow my life apart again or drive me out of my mind, neither of which I want to ever face."

Rachelle sat up straight in her chair. "This is serious business, isn't it?"

"Yes it is serious and that's not all of it."

"There's more?"

"Oh yes, there's more. There was a picture of Bobby in my house, sitting on my bed with a note attached to it." Teyona paraphrased the content of the note.

"Damn!" Rachelle exclaimed.

"Yeah, right."

"Someone is really mad at you, girl. Something like that would definitely make me shit my pants."

Teyona smiled weakly, "I'm right there with you."

"Do you have no idea who could be doing this? I mean wouldn't someone have to have access to your home? Even if it was some trick photography to pose you and Bobby together at certain places where you know you two never were, how could a picture of the inside of your house be available to them?" Rachelle was more than a little concern now. "Are you going to go to the police?"

"I don't know." Teyona shrugged. "I wouldn't know what to say to them, that I've got pictures of a dead man in my house long after the man was dead? Someone is playing a terrible trick on me about something that happened in the past. It's not so much that I want to protect myself as I want to protect Steven. I can't put him through something like that again. I can't."

"This is awful. It seems like someone is definitely out to get you. What are you gonna do, Teyona?" Rachelle said, with concern in her voice and on her face.

"I wish I could answer that." Teyona said, looking off into space.

"I wish there was something I could do to help."

"You have. I feel better just being able to talk with someone about what I'm going through and you listened. Sometimes that's enough."

An hour later, Teyona and Rachelle left the spa. Teyona knew talking to Rachelle couldn't solve her problems, but she felt some sense of relief just being able to talk about her problems with someone who would listen to her and not judge her. Rachelle was that person and had been for years.

Teyona was driving home when suddenly a car appeared to have come out of nowhere, hitting her car and sending her careening into another vehicle. The EMS staffers arrived quickly removing her from her car and onto a waiting stretcher and she felt excruciating pain shoot through her leg as they did so. The ambulance transported her to the hospital where she was immediately taken in to have X-rays done. Steven had arrived while she was in X-ray and she could see the worry on his face as he rushed over to her. An emergency doctor informed them that Teyona had a broken ankle. They planned only for her to remain in the hospital overnight for observation but as it turned out, she stayed in the hospital for two days with Steven never leaving her side. He took off from work a week to take care of Teyona while she became acclimated to the crutches to get around.

Before going back to work that Monday morning, Steven made breakfast for them. He made sure that Teyona had everything she needed before leaving the house. He called his office and had his appointments pushed back later so he could go to the Mercedes dealership purchase her a new car and have it delivered to their house. Steven arranged with their housekeeper to check in on Teyona daily to make sure she didn't need anything.

Teyona put the breakfast dishes into the dishwasher and went into the den to do some ankle exercises. Upon hearing her doorbell rang, she grabbed her crutches and limped slowly down the hall and through the foyer to answer the door. Opening the door was her last memory before coming to. Opening her eyes, she found herself lying on the couch in her den, unaware of how she got there, and Bobby Johnson staring at her from across the room in Steven's lazy-boy.   Seeing Teyona coming around, the man tossed the magazine aside that he'd been leafing through. She placed her feet on the floor and tried to stand, grimacing as the pain ripped through her ankle, then she sat and pulled herself up into a sitting position on the couch. Again she tried standing up but dizziness overcame her and she settled down again.

The Bobby Johnson's look-a-like uncrossed his legs, pulled himself to the edge of his seat and asked in a sadistic tone, "Did you enjoy fucking my brother?"

It took a moment for the words to wrap themselves around Teyona's brain. "Who are you?" she demanded. "What are you doing in my house?" It was as if she were experiencing déjà vu all over again. She slowly got up from the couch, looking around for her crutches, which she didn't see. She put most of her weight on her stronger ankle and facing the stranger who sat comfortably in her house, she said, "I want you to leave my home!"

He ignored her order. He just sat there watching her and repeated his original question, "Did you enjoy fucking my brother?" He leaned towards her, hissing his words. "Which did you like most; fucking my brother or killing him?"

Teyona waved her hand furiously for him to go. "I said I want you to leave my house. Get out now!"

"Why? Am I not welcome here?" He reclined a little back into the chair. His tone was harsh and his eyes flashed with fury. "You didn't have a problem allowing my brother in, did you?"

"Who are you?"

"Although I think you know who I am, I'm gonna even the playing field and tell you exactly who I am. I am Russell Andrew Johnson. Bobby Addison Johnson was my twin brother."

She dropped back down hard on the couch. "It was you," she said in a whisper.

"Excuse me," he said gazing at her, but knowing exactly what she was referring to.

"It was you at the art show a few weeks ago."

"Yes. It was me." He was matter of fact.

"Why didn't you say something? Do you have any idea how much you upset me that night?"

His voice rose, his head jerked and he angrily spat out at her, "Am I supposed to care about upsetting you when you gunned down my brother like he was some kind of animal?" He clenched his fist tightly, "Have you any idea how that has upset me, affected me?"

"I want you to leave." Teyona raised her voice.

Russell again reclined in the seat, his voice became calmer and he shook his head. "Nah, I ain't leaving until I find out everything I need to know about you and my brother. From how you two came to know each other to how he ended up dead in your home, in your bedroom," Russell said looking around. "I understand you moved to this place after that tragic night."

"I don't own you an explanation, number one and number two, if you don't get out of here in the next minute, I'm gonna call the police and have you arrested for breaking into my home."

Russell wasn't fazed by Teyona's threat of calling the police. "You can call whoever you want but I'm not leaving until I get what I came for."

She glanced at her watch. "Look, my husband will be home anytime now and I don't want you here when he gets home."

Russell harrumphed and smiled knowingly. He knew there was no chance that the good doctor would be coming home any time soon. Hell, the good doc was probably getting it on with one of his nurses or the fine black chick, but he said, "Then you had better start talking."He smiled again but this smile held no warmth.

Russell was in town to get the story about his brother, as they say, from the horse's mouth and he intended to learn everything that happened with his brother and when he did, he'd make someone pay!

Teyona sat back down on the couch and put both hands up to her mouth. "I never knew Bobby had a twin."

Russell eyes narrowed as he watched her. "Did you ever want to know anything about him except to get what you wanted?" His voice was ice cold. "Did you try to find out the kind of person he was, things he like to do, his favorite food, his favorite color? Did you know anything about my brother other than how he screwed you?" His eyes pierced into hers.

She looked at Russell Johnson, Bobby's brother. He looked like Bobby, had his handsome face and muscular body but he was much more sophisticated, spoke differently, dressed differently, more suave. "You're right. I didn't know Bobby very well, except in the beginning, I liked him. He was fun, spontaneous, and he made me laugh. I liked being with him. "

"For sex, you mean."

She swallowed hard. "Yes. It was just sex. I really didn't want him to care about me either. You see, Mr. Johnson, I love my husband very much and he loves me more than anything. When Bobby and I got together, it really wasn't supposed to happen. I wasn't looking for anyone. I especially wasn't looking for anyone to fall in love with me. When we got involved, I was lonely and I wanted sex. I needed it. It was nothing more than that but somewhere along the way, Bobby's feelings changed, he wanted more from me. . ." Teyona began and she didn't stop talking until she'd told Russell the entire story: from the day Bobby returned to her home, made love to her there to the night he broke into her home to kill her and her husband. "Your brother was a nice man and he was nice to me in a strange kind of way."

"What do you mean?"

"He was very rude in the way he talked to me, almost vulgar at times, but strangely enough, after a while, I didn't mind it. As a matter of fact, I thought the way he expressed himself suited him. He was just being true to himself." Teyona stopped talking for a moment, looking down at her hands that were clamped in her lap. Then, looking up again, she said, "I'm sorry about what happened to your brother. I'm so sorry."

"You are sorry about killing my brother, you mean."

Teyona didn't respond to that comment.

Suddenly, Russell got up from his seat. "What time are you free tomorrow?"

She was surprised by the question. Was he planning to pay her another visit? "Why?" She asked.

"Because I'd like to talk with you some more about my brother," he answered, "but I would like to come at a time when it's convenient for you."

She answered slowly. "Would eleven in the morning be good for you?"

"Eleven is fine with me." Russell turned to leave and Teyona was about to get up also, but he lifted a hand to stop her. "Don't bother, I will show myself out, and I would appreciate it if you didn't tell anyone that I was here." With that, he left. She didn't get up again until she heard her front door closed. She limped over to her crutches and made it to the front window to see Russell's car turning out of her driveway.

The next morning, Russell arrived at Teyona's house promptly at eleven o'clock. After confronting the woman who killed his brother, he was so spent that he stopped off at Cleo's and got something to eat before returning to his hotel, with even more unanswered questions revolving around inside his head.

138

Teyona answered the door, Russell entered and he couldn't help thinking how beautiful she was. She offered him coffee which he accepted and they went directly into the kitchen. She poured two cups of coffee and set them on the table. "Can I get you something to go with your coffee? We have muffins."

"No coffee is fine, thank you."

She sat across from Russell and remained quiet while he talked. He asked a number of questions and when he repeated a question and she mentioned it, he acknowledged he was aware but just wanted to hear as much as he could about his brother anyway. They talked a couple of hours and Teyona noticed that the more she and Russell Johnson talked, the more comfortable they became. The tension began to peel away, layer by layer until after a while, they began to talk like they'd known each other for a long time. As they revealed more about Bobby Johnson and even more about themselves, Teyona saw Russell's eyes brighten. She wasn't sure whether it was with the anger she knew consumed him or tears she thought he was on the verge of releasing. She found herself feeling compassion for him. What she said next caught Russell by surprise. "Mr. Johnson, tell me about Bobby, please," she said and asked, "What was he really like?"

Russell looked at her. He could see the strain on her face and he knew it all wasn't because he was there. He knew the recent pictures she'd received had caused her some stress. As he continued to look

139

at her, he didn't know what to make of this woman. Initially he was consumed with thoughts of hurting her physically and emotionally with pain that would last a lifetime but now he was beginning to experience something else entirely. He was beginning to feel this was a woman who got caught up in circumstances because sexual needs weren't being met at home. Russell understood now just why Dr. Teyona Carter might have gotten involved with his brother and why his brother got involved with her. For he couldn't help being aware of the most uncomfortable erection slowly bulging against his trousers just by looking at this woman and listening to her voice. "What do you want to know?" he queried.

"Anything you can tell me."

"Bobby," Russell began looking for the right words, "was a good kid, different than a lot of people, like doing things his way whether anyone like it or not." Russell chuckled and continued, "He was always getting into trouble in school, with the folks. They had no idea how to handle him. On one hand, he was this super kid but Bobby could also be difficult."

"Were the two of you close?"

"Yeah," he looked wistfully, "we were, then we weren't, then we were on the path of becoming close again." Russell explained seeing a confused expression on Teyona's face, "Bobby and I had a falling out about five years ago. Before we could resolve our issue, he left Detroit, came here and we didn't speak again until a month before, he was killed." He still wanted his words to hurt Teyona. He couldn't allow her to go free and with a clear conscious after killing someone who was a part of him.

"Mind if I ask what was it that caused the split between the two of you?"

"You really need to ask?" Russell raised an eyebrow and chuckled again, "What else? A woman. I got involved with a woman who he was involved with."

"I am sure that would be reason enough to cause something like that to happen."

"Only I didn't know he was seeing her. Bobby dated so many women that it was difficult to keep up with them. I'd just come home from Iraq and as you might imagine, I was back in the States, thrilled to be alive and buck wild, hitting everything that wore a skirt," he disclosed. "I was in a club one night and Bobby well he had this night job so he was at work. The two of us were to meet up later at the club but as it turned out, one of his girls came in. She didn't tell me she was with Bobby. I didn't know her, but she had to know me. Bobby and I are identical twins. Long story short, we left the club together, went to a hotel and when I dropped her off the next morning, Bobby was sitting on her porch waiting for her. As it turned out, Bobby lost it, he punched me in the face, split with his girl and left town two days later. He kept in touch with our parents but he wouldn't talk to me or answer any of my calls or texts. Weeks turned into months, then years. It wasn't until a little over a year ago that he contacted me. After that time, we spoke every day. We reconnected and I was happy to have my little brother back in my life."

"Your little brother?"

"Well yeah, I was born six minutes ahead of him." Russell flashed an awkward grin.

Teyona smiled also.

"I wish I had come here when he asked me too, I might have been able to prevent him from doing some of the things he did. Could've possibly saved his life. When I learned that my brother had been killed in some couple's house, along with all the dirty details of what he intended to do to you and your husband, I lost it."

"I wonder why didn't Bobby tell me he had a twin?" She allowed herself to ask the question again.

"Bobby had his own way of doing things. We weren't the good twin, bad twin. He just always did things differently." Russell paused before saying, "I'm sure he would've told you he had a twin and a lot more had you been interested."

Teyona believed what Russell said was true. There were often times when Bobby tried to talk with her, but she would discourage it. She asked, "How long have you been in town?"

"A while."

"Oh." She accepted his non-informational response.

"Will you be staying a while or returning to Detroit?"

"That depends."

Russell quickly thought about it, then he decided to answer her questions. "I've been here a couple of months and actually, I have no idea how long I'll stay. Until I wrap things up, I imagine."

"What have you been doing? I mean, you seem to know a lot about me. You have been investigating me, haven't you?"

"You could say that," he replied, then added, sadly, "My brother came here looking for a fresh start. I just wish things had turned out differently for him."

"So do I, Russell. So do I," she replied, a little above a whisper.

Russell Johnson stared at Teyona. How was it that his feelings for her had so easily done a three sixty. She didn't appear to be the woman he thought she was or was she cunning enough to fool him? Had she deceived his brother? Russell wasn't sure but he still intended to find out. As he stared at her, he wondered how she was going to receive the information about her husband's cheating ways but more importantly, who he was cheating with? Russell's instinct about people was very keen. He'd always been told that his intuition was spot on. "I'd like to talk with you again, if that's alright with you," he said, looking away from her, suddenly unable to look her in her eye. He believed she'd been completely honest with him but he was withholding information from her.

Without giving it a second thought, Teyona replied, "That's fine."

Russell rose up out of his seat. He held out his hand and helped her to stand with her crutches. They walked together to the front door, said their goodbyes and as Russell was about to walk away, he looked deeply into her eyes and said, "Take care of yourself."

For a moment, all Teyona saw was Bobby Johnson and she felt a slight chill run the course of her body. "And you as well," she heard herself say. She watched him scrunch up his jacket around his neck and begin walking down the steps toward his car. The conversation between Teyona and Russell had been so intense: opening old wounds, learning about each other and her learning more about Bobby, that she hadn't notice it had begun to rain.

Russell got to the final step before touching pavement when he turned back to her. His voice carried loudly over the falling rain, "I'd still like us to keep these visits between the two of us. Will you promise me that?"

"I don't like lying to my husband or my friends."

"Just hold off for a little longer. For now, please don't tell anyone that I was here or that you and I have been in contact. Promise me that."

Teyona looked at him, confused and thinking what an odd request, she thought. "I don't know whether I can make that promise," she confessed.

"I'm not asking you to do it for me. I'm asking you to do it for Bobby and yourself."

What an odd thing for Russell to say, she thought, yet there was something so compelling in his eyes that she wanted to do as he'd asked. "You must have your reasons for asking me to do that. Do you care to share with me?"

"I do have my reasons and you will know it all in due time," Russell said, walking away, leaving her more confused than ever. She was not in a hurry to let her husband know that the brother of her former lover had been sitting in their home, not once but twice, having conversations with her about his dead brother. But, how much longer could she last not telling Rachelle what had been going on? She told Rachelle everything, she always had.

Teyona closed the door after Russell and on her crutches, was making her way back to the den when, suddenly she heard the door to the kitchen open and in walked Steven carrying his briefcase.

"I just realized it's raining," she said, wondering whether Steven saw Russell leaving their home.

"Yes, it's pouring," Steven answered and asked, "Who was that leaving as I was coming in?"

"That was Russell Andrew," she replied, deliberately omitting Russell's last name, yet not sure why but was relieved knowing Steven hadn't gotten a good look at him. If he had, he certainly would've recognized him.

"What was he doing here?"

"He's trying to work through some things, he wanted to talk and since I won't be back in the office for a while, I made an exception."

"You think it's a good idea to have your patients come to our home?"

"It's not the best idea but he really needed to talk." Teyona changed the subject. "You're home early."

"I wanted to come home and check on you," Steven said, then added, "You seem edgy, not like yourself. You want to tell me what that's about?"

CHAPTER 15

RUSSELL

In his car driving away from Teyona's house, Russell picked up his phone and dialed a number. When the call connected, he said, "Don't send any more pictures. As a matter of fact, don't do anything until you hear further from me." Russell listened before he spoke again. "Cute." He paused, irritated. "I said no more pictures." He waited and listened again. "You can fuck him as long as you want but I don't want you sending any more pictures to her. You got that?" He listened. "That's none of your business what I'm feeling, you just follow instructions." With that, Russell ended the call, threw the phone down on the seat and as he sped down the street, he said, "No class bitch."

Russell had met that crazy bitch by accident when he arrived six months ago. He'd been conducting an investigation and at the end of the day, he went to have some dinner. Leaving the restaurant, he came face to face with her. She recognized his face, told him so and began to ask a lot of questions. One thing led to another and they agreed to join forces to work together to take down the one responsible for killing his brother. It took very little for Russell to convince her to help. Truthfully, she was overly eager and excited to help him which made him wonder about the kind of woman she really was. Red flags went up and although he knew he couldn't trust her, she still could be useful to him. Working with her, she had proved her usefulness but now he was relinquishing her services. He didn't need her anymore.

CHAPTER 16

STEVEN

Unaware that he was being followed, Steven was in route to the Magnolia Suites where he was going to meet someone of the female persuasion for an early evening tryst before going home to the woman he truly loved, his wife. As he carefully and expertly drove through the Friday evening traffic, his mind recalled the guilt that covered Teyona's face daily when he looked at her and her eyes greeted his. He knew what she was thinking and he purposely allowed her to think it. Why couldn't he have been a little less judgmental of her when he was doing the same himself, more in fact? Teyona didn't know and he hoped she'd never find out that he'd always had a woman or more accurately, women on the side. Over the years, Steven had had so many affairs that he could've actually been referred to as a sex addict. He'd just been cunning enough to not get caught, to keep his dirty, steamy little secrets hidden. And, he'd been good at it. He loved his wife, there was never any doubt about that but one woman could never be enough for him. He was one of those men who enjoyed a variety. He wasn't sure how long the craving for other women would last but until the urge stopped, he would continue to enjoy it. Steven was sure his wife would never cheat on him again. He would make sure that he did or said things that would make her feel so guilty that she would willingly toe the line.

Steven pulled into a parking space on the side of the hotel, exited his car and walked swiftly through the entry door of the hotel. He went directly to the bank of elevators, pressed the UP button and was joined by three others; a Caucasian couple, or a man with one of his side pieces, and an African American man with a full beard and a cap identifying a pizza business, pulled down covering most of his face. He was carrying a large pizza box in his hands.

The delivery man glanced briefly at Steven. The man looked vaguely familiar; a patient at some time or perhaps a caddy at the club. Steven wasn't sure; only he felt he'd seen that man somewhere before. "Looks like someone has the right idea," he said to the delivery man.

"Looks that way," the pizza man replied, glancing briefly into Stevens eyes before casting his eyes back down on the box he was carrying. When the elevator doors opened, they all entered, Steven pressed the desired floor as did the others. The doors opened, Steven and the delivery man exited the elevator on the same floor and walked in the same direction down the corridor. Steven softly knocked on the third door from the elevator while the delivery man whistled softly as he walked on down the hall. Within moments, the door to the suite opened to allow Steven to enter. He was greeted by a gorgeous woman wearing a sheer black negligee that revealed all her feminine assets.

Steven pulled her roughly to him as her red lips curled in laughter. In the seconds that followed, their bodies molded together, Rachelle wrapped her arms tightly around his neck and greeted him with a passionate and sensuous kiss, stabbing her tongue deeply into his mouth, seeking his and immediately began dueling. While heat instantly licked at her body causing her most intimate spot to begin to moisten, she could feel the stretch of his manhood as it came to life, grinding against her mid-section.

As the kiss intensified, Steven reached down and began to caress her between her beautiful, brown thighs. He slid his fingers underneath the thin, flimsy layer of fabric that covered a small portion of her womanhood and caressed her there, his fingers mingling with her wet slick curls. He was thrilled he was able to evoke such a rapid response from her. He pushed one finger into her, then two, then three. She began to grind against his fingers. It wasn't long before he had eased his entire hand inside her and began to grant her startling pleasure. Momentarily, he removed his hand from her and lifted a finger up to his mouth to taste what she was so eager for him to have.

Rachelle pulled Steven's coat down his arms and tossed it on a chair and began to unbutton his shirt, then unzipped his pants. After his pants and underwear were around his ankles, she dropped to her knees, took his very formidable erection into both hands and licked her lips before she put it into her mouth. She enclosed her mouth around his rock hard penis and moved on it, taking several inches inside her mouth. She held it in her hot, wet mouth without any movement. Then, she pulled back and began to lick, nibble and suck his tip, sending repeating spasms throughout his body. Steven moved his hips around, back and forth, sending his penis against the back of her throat, where she began to suck on him, furiously. As his knees began to weaken, he reached down, placed his hands under her arms and snatched her from the floor, lifting her up in his arms and effortlessly, carried her over to the bed.

Both completely naked now and on the bed, Steven's hands moved up and down Rachelle's voluptuous body and as he kissed her, plunging his tongue into her mouth, she responded in kind. His mouth left hers and moved to her full, firm breasts. He took one of the swollen dark nipples into his mouth and feasted upon it. He bit and sucked on it so fiercely that she let out a loud moan. He inserted his penis at her slick, hot center and shoved hard into her. In the next second, he was plunging into her zestfully, furiously, relentlessly. He glanced down at her. In his haze, he couldn't miss the odd expression on her face; her top lip was pulled back, exposing her teeth as though she was grinning at him, her nose flared, her eyes ablaze.

Steven pumped powerfully into Rachelle and as her eyes rolled back into her head, they came together in a thunderous, astounding climax, and then, he rolled off of her. Gasping for air, he piled his pillows and reclining in bed, he placed one arm under his head and the other across his chest.

"We've got to stop this," he said, pulling air into his lungs, without looking at Rachelle.

"What do you mean?" she asked, breathing hard, looking over at him.

"This is the second time that we've been together this week. I don't want us to get sloppy and get caught, for both our asses will be in trouble."

"Why are you worrying about that now?"

"I just don't want us to get too comfortable and end up in a bad situation."

"Like Teyona?" Rachelle threw out.

That remark upset Steven. "No, not Teyona. As a matter of fact what we're doing has little to do with Teyona. I just don't want us to fuck up, okay?"

"And how long have we been doing this now?" she asked and answered her own question. "Three years, I believe, and you think now all of a sudden that we should stop seeing each other? Aren't you forgetting something?"

"No, I'm not forgetting anything. You know I will take care of my responsibilities."

"I know that but what about me? I'm not ready to end what we have."

"Speaking of Teyona, not only do I not like doing this to her and with her friend no less, aren't you afraid you will let something slip? Teyona is not a stupid woman, you know."

"Really? How smart can she be to not have any idea that we're banging each other every chance we get? Talk about clueless. That non-stupid woman would be so out of her element trying to outsmart me." Rachelle leaned over, kissed Steven on his mouth and said, "She really is clueless, you know. If George was having sex with someone else, I'd know about it. We're supposed to know these things." Rachelle rolled her eyes. "Our bodies communicate, our bodies tell us things but it's too bad if we have our heads stuck so deep in the sand that we just don't see it." Rachelle shrugged her shoulders. "Anyway, it's her own damn fault."

Steven ignored what she said. "You should try to get back on the same page as George. . .," he was saying before he was interrupted.

"Why? Are you seeing someone else?"

Steven gave her a look. "Where did that come from?"

"You didn't answer me."

"You know I'm not seeing anyone else," he lied. "How could that be when I have a tiger like you in bed with me whenever I want you?"

Rachelle smiled, pleased with what she felt was a compliment.

"Call it what you want but sometimes I find myself feeling a little guilty." Steven ran a hand down his face. "It may just be that I'm getting old and want to put some order in my life."

"Hardly." She reached down under the sheet and began to fondle him. "I bet I can make you forget all about the guilt you're feeling."

"I don't think so," he replied in annoyance. "Teyona is a good woman, a decent woman who doesn't deserve what we're doing to her. You know that. Hell, she made a mistake like so many of us do. She's human. We all make mistakes, but she'd never betray me the way I'm betraying her. She would never fuck around with one of my friend and she definitely wouldn't fuck her best friend's husband."

"So now you're trying to make me feel like shit?"

"No, not at all," Steven said, reaching up and scratched the side of his head.

"So what are you saying? Because I'm screwing my best friend's husband, that makes me more of a no good, whoring ass, bitch than she? I don't think so." In a huff, Rachelle moved away from Steven and folded both arms across her chest.

Steven ignored her comment. "Knock it off, Rachelle," he said, angrily. "You're reading too much into this." He paused a moment and placed both hands under his head. "Sometimes when I look at her, I can see the regret, the guilt all over her. She doesn't deserve to feel that way. I don't blame her totally for what she did. I wasn't there for her the way I should have been, coming home late every night, not spending the kind of time with her that she deserved. She was lonely and found what she needed elsewhere." For an instant, he looked remorseful. "Teyona really is a terrific woman. . ."

"I don't want to hear one more time about what a great and terrific woman Teyona is," Rachelle interrupted him. "Do you think for one second Teyona was feeling guilty when she couldn't keep her ass away from Bobby Johnson, fucking his eyeballs out of his head every chance she got? Well no, she didn't! She couldn't wait to run off to meet that young buck and screw him half the night, getting her whims satisfied before running back home to you, acting all sweet and innocent," she snarled, but Steven remembered that time well. Teyona had changed. She went through a period when she didn't act her normal happy self. It didn't occur to him until after the affair was over and Bobby Johnson was dead that that was the reason for the change in her behavior. Teyona had been feeling guilty long before the affair with Bobby Johnson was over. "You don't owe Dr. Teyona Carter a damn thing," Rachelle stormed, interrupting his reverie. "Nothing!"

Steven looked at Rachelle as if for the first time since they'd been seeing each other. He saw something in her eyes that he'd not seen before; something hateful, something evil. Did Rachelle hate Teyona? Could she actually hate her that much?

An hour later, Steven had showered, dressed and was on his way home.

Ten minutes later, from behind the steering wheel of his car in the Magnolia Suites parking lot, Russell watched Rachelle as she exited the hotel. She walked across the parking lot, climbed into her car and drove away.

"That bitch," he said, raising a hand to rub his forehead. He'd waited in the parking lot for Steven to come out, took pictures of him and now Rachelle. He had a gut feeling that whoever Steven was seeing at the hotel that night would be leaving shortly after him. Russell scanned the pictures in his phone, sending them to the printer he had set up back at the hotel and drove away.

CHAPTER 17

TEYONA & RUSSELL

One week later, Russell called Teyona.

"This is Dr. Carter," she answered, apprehensively.

"I'd like to see you."

"What did you want to see me about?" Teyona asked.

"I'd like to talk with you." Russell paused. "Talking with you helps me process what my brother may have been going through. I hope you can give me a little time today," he said and quickly asked, "Do you have some time today? It doesn't matter what time you can see me. I just need to see you as soon as I can."

Teyona detected the urgency in Russell's voice. She'd been back at work and no longer needed the crutches but still had a slight limp and wore flat shoes. She pushed a piece of hair from her face, locked it behind her ear and looked at her watch. It was eleven forty-five in the morning. She checked her calendar. Her next patient was scheduled to arrive at one. "I have another patient coming in about an hour or so. How soon can you get here? I can have my assistant show you right in."

"I'll be there shortly."

Russell arrived at Teyona's office within five minutes, carrying a manila envelope in his hand and was shown in immediately. He couldn't get over how gorgeous Teyona was and looking very professional wearing a dark suit and white blouse; however, there was an uneasiness that covered her entire body. Russell wondered why. Although it'd happened relatively quickly, he thought they'd established a relationship where they felt comfortable with each other, but what had happened to change that? Was she still skeptical of him? She offered him a seat across from her desk. "That was fast. You must've been nearby."

"Right down the street," he admitted.

"I see. So, Mr. Johnson, what did you want to talk with me about?"

"You seem uncomfortable. I thought I detected something in your voice when I called. Is something wrong?"

"I'm fine, but I believe you came here to talk about yourself," she slapped her hands on her desk and in her most professional voice, said, "Why don't we get started."

Russell blinked. "I can see that something is bothering you so why not run it by me. Maybe I can help. I know you are the therapist and all but sometimes someone outside the situation might be able to shed a different light on whatever it is that's going on with you."

Teyona looked at him, thoughtfully. She took a deep breath. "Perhaps you're right," she said softly, wringing her hands. "A short while ago, someone sent me pictures of your brother, or someone who looks like your brother. I received more of the same pictures last night. I have no idea who is doing this to me or what to do about it, for that matter. If your hair was longer, I would've thought it was you in the pictures," she said, relaying to him how receiving those pictures had affected her. "I can't confide in my husband because I don't want him to return to the past and all that happened back then. I just want us to forget the past and move forward."

"That bitch," Russell exclaimed under his breath. He'd made it perfectly clear to his contact that no additional pictures were to be sent to Teyona. Now he was going to have to check her.

"You said something?"

"No," Russell covered quickly, "just listening and thinking how awful that must be for you. Sometimes the best thing to do in a situation like that is nothing. It's probably someone who knows you. If you start to freak out and they see that, then they'll have some leverage over you and you don't ever want to give someone the upper hand on your life. For the moment, just don't do anything and see how long this goes on. Very often if you ignore a situation, the perpetrators will give up and move on to another target. Hopefully that doesn't happen but

160

don't do anything and see it if all just doesn't go away."

Teyona nodded in agreement.

After she'd calmed down, Russell asked, "How did my brother seem the night he died?!"

Teyona felt relieved that Russell didn't say the night she killed him. "He seemed distraught, highly agitated. Different than I'd ever seen him."

"You told me in our past conversations that there were times when Bobby would become very upset with you about something he wanted from you that you were unwilling to give."

"Yes."

"Why didn't he try to hurt you one of those times? What happened to cause him to do what he did that particular night?" Russell wanted to know.

Teyona knew what caused Bobby to lose control at that time. Yes, he'd been angry at her for rejecting him but was really infuriated by Steven going to his job, calling him out and embarrassing him in front of his co-workers, threatening bodily harm if he went near his wife again. Closing her eyes briefly, she took a deep, measured breath to steady her nerves, and said, "When Steven found out about our affair, he went to see Bobby at his job and there were some threats made. Those threats were made in front of Bobby's co-workers. It angered Bobby to the point where he must've lost it. That evening, Steven and I went out to dinner and came home to find Bobby waiting for us, in our bedroom. I've already told you what he intended to do to us."

"Tell me again!" Russell urged.

Teyona looked at Russell. She'd already repeated that story to Russell a number of times and the last thing she wanted to do was rehash that night again but she felt she owed Bobby's brother some peace of mind, some closure and if that was what it took, she'd do it. "As you know, he chloroformed Steven and tied him up."

"Go on! I wanna know what he said exactly, what was his demeanor like."

"Bobby was different that night. I had never seen him like that, ever."

"In what way?"

Teyona looked down at her hands on top of her desk. She stumbled over her first few words, recalling that painful night, "Bobby, he looked, he looked like. . . like he hadn't slept in days or had bathed. His hair was grown out more than usual and looked as though it hadn't been combed in a while. His beard wasn't neatly trimmed as he had always worn it." Teyona paused momentarily to look out the window in her office. "So unlike the usual Bobby."

"What did he say to you and *your husband*," Russell asked and Teyona could tell he'd said the words '*your husband*' with unchecked disdain.

She returned her attention to Russell. "He said he was going to have sex with me in our bed, with my husband watching." She paused again. "Then, he said after he finished with me, he was going to cut off my husband's testicles and ram them down his throat, just as Steven had threatened to do to him."

162

"It seems to me that you were collateral damage."

Teyona didn't reply. She just stared at Russell.

"I believe although it would've been difficult for Bobby, extremely difficult, he would've honored your decision to end the relationship but when Dr. Steven got involved and embarrassed him in the presence of others, that's what pissed him off, causing him to go crazy." Russell got up from his chair, rubbing his hand along his chin as he walked over to the window and looked out. Teyona remained quiet, gave him time to assess what he needed to. She couldn't deny what Russell was saying to be true. She'd even thought the same many times herself.

Russell returned to his seat. "Once when we were early teens, Bobby got into a fight with another kid at school. As long as it was between the two of them, things were fine, everything was okay but when the kid threatened Bobby with bodily harm and said some really embarrassing things to him, Bobby went insane. He broke the kid's nose, an arm and the boy's parents threatened to sue my parents. It was resolved after a number of talks between our parents and the boy's parents." Russell shook his head reliving that awful ordeal that'd happened years ago.

He and Teyona continued to talk until the buzzer sounded on her phone on the desk. She looked at her watch. One o'clock on the dot. "My one o'clock is here," she said.

Russell stood up. He extended a hand to her. That gesture surprised her, but she lifted her hand to his. "Thank you for seeing me. I'm sure I'll want to see you again," he said.

"I expect as much. These talks help me as well. You seem to understand the situation without being judgmental more than anyone."

Russell left Teyona's office. He went out to the underground parking lot, got into his car and dropped the envelope on the passenger's seat. He'd intended sharing with Teyona, all that he'd learned about that lying, cheating, snobbish ass of a man she so proudly called *her husband*, but he'd wait. He still felt that there was more for him to learn, but first things first.

Russell made a phone call. "Meet me at the spot, NOW!" he said and hung up.

He drove to the meeting place and entered the abandoned building. Seeing his contact, he said before she reached him, "Bitch, didn't I tell you not to send Dr. Carter any more pictures?"

His contact snickered and said, "I couldn't resist doing it one last time. She freaked so badly the first time it did my heart good to know that these would send her ass over the moon."

Russell grabbed her by her arm and jerked her to him. "Wad up with you? Did you not understand what I told you?"

"I understood what you said," she admitted. He held her arm tightly a moment longer before he released it.

"Don't let me hear that you have done that again. Am I making myself clear?"

When Rachelle didn't respond, he asked again very forcefully, "I said am I making myself clear, damn it?"

"Yes," Rachelle responded, her eyes popping wide open.

"I don't intend to be having this conversation with you again." Russell gave Rachelle a cold, hard stare.

"You won't," Rachelle replied, then she added, "I don't know what kind of spell you have put on her anyway or her on you for that matter. She usually can't wait to tell me everything that's going on with her, but she still hasn't told me you two have been in contact. And here you are, looking out for her, kissing her ass instead of driving her fucking ass over a cliff. What's up with that?"

"What I do is none of your business. You just do what you're told. No more, no less. You got that?"

"Yes. Good grief, I get it, okay. What is it about Teyona that everyone wants to protect her? I hate that bitch."

"Do you think for one second that I don't know that? You've made that abundantly clear." He pointed a finger at her. "You just do what you're told and you'd better be careful. Your own little shit could be exposed."

CHAPTER 18

TEYONA & RACHELLE

Rachelle called Teyona and they'd agreed to meet at The Olive Garden on Two Notch Road for dinner. Teyona arrived looking magnificent, wearing a soft floral summer dress that fell a little above her knees and nicely against her feminine curves. Her medium blue strappy heels and purse picked up the dominant blue in the dress. A gold bracelet and watch completed her outfit. Teyona was about to enter the restaurant when Rachelle pulled up and waved to her happily as she parked. She got out of the car looking fabulous as well dressed in a pale yellow sleeveless top, matching slacks and black shoes and purse. A pair of diamond earrings hung from her earlobes and a matching bracelet adorned her wrist.

The women embraced at the door before entering the restaurant. Once they were seated and ordered dinner and a glass of wine each, Teyona said, "What did you want to talk about? I'm usually the one who needs to talk." She grinned at her friend. "It must be serious."

Rachelle was hoping that Teyona would share with her about her secret rendezvous with Russell. She always told Rachelle everything but now she was keeping secrets and Rachelle didn't like it, but she said, "It is serious. I'm burned out and I need a break. I was thinking about getting out of town for a few days and enjoy some sun, some fun, you know, escapism, paradise, like a Disneyland for adults."

Teyona was thinking with all that she'd been through lately, she could use some away time herself. "I like the sound of that but where are you thinking about going and when?"

"One of the islands like Ocho Rios or the Bahamas, within the next week or two. Anywhere, just away from here for a minute."

"Are we taking the boys with us?"

"That would be up to them."

"And how long are you planning to stay?"

"Only a few days. Just long enough to push the stress back a little."

They chuckled together.

The waitress brought each a glass of wine and water before leaving the table again.

"I'll run it by Steven and see what he wants to do. Will George be up for it, just starting his new business and all?"

"I haven't mentioned it to him yet."

"What are you waiting on to mention a trip to your husband? If you expect him to go, he's going to need time to work things out with the people at the office."

"That's his problem."

167

"What?" Teyona was incredulous.

"Chile, please," Rachelle said with a wave of her hand. "If he can't handle his business and line things up in a couple of weeks, well, bye Felicia."

The waitress brought each woman a pasta dish, green salad and bread sticks, and they began to eat. "I'm going to tell you something but I don't want you to ask any questions. I'll tell you more as soon as I figure this whole thing out," Rachelle stated.

"Okay," Teyona replied slowly as she raised a fork of salad to her mouth.

"I'm in love," Rachelle announced, stuffing a fork of pasta into her mouth as she glanced over at Teyona to see her reaction.

Teyona's head snapped up. "Did you just say you're in love? With George, I hope." She took a sip from her water glass.

"No, not with George." Rachelle clicked her teeth, giving Teyona a dark look. "George? Chile, please."

"Then what are you talking about? Who with? Are you having an affair again?" The questions tumbled out of a surprised Teyona's mouth.

"You could say that," she calmly bit off a piece of bread.

"What? That you're having an affair? Why would you do that again? We've talked about this, Rachelle and agreed that we would never go down that road again. You know the results could be as disastrous for you as they were for me."

"I believe I told you that I didn't want any questions, besides, I can have a secret too if I want to since there're plenty secrets going around," Rachelle said, giving Teyona a look before shoving more food into her mouth. "Anyway, I wouldn't put it past you to get involved with another man again as well." If Teyona got involved with Bobby Johnson, his brother Russell, was a real ladies man, she thought.

"You've got to be kidding."

"Really?"

"Rachelle, you can't be serious."

"I'm one hundred percent serious. Speaking of getting involved with another man other than your husband, have you had any more Bobby Johnson's look-a-like sightings?"

"What is that supposed to mean?" Teyona avoided answering the question. "If I see the man who resembles Bobby Johnson again, I am supposed to have an affair with him? Is that what you're saying?"

"Stranger things have happened."

Teyona laid her fork across her plate and looked at Rachelle. Could she know that she and Russell have been meeting and talking? She asked, "What's going on with you, woman? You've been behaving so unlike yourself. Is there something you want to tell me?"

Rachelle gave Teyona a cunning look and asked, "Like what?"

"I don't know. I haven't said anything but I have noticed a change in you."

"We've got to mix it up a little, honey. Evolution is the name of the game," Rachelle said, taking a sip from her wineglass.

Teyona looked at Rachelle a long while before she shrugged her shoulders and resumed eating. She wouldn't force the issue. Rachelle did indicate she'd tell her more when she knew more. She'd just wait. And, if Rachelle knew that she'd been communicating with Russell, she didn't say and neither would Teyona.

More than an hour later, Teyona and Rachelle left the restaurant and went home.

She had kept her word and hadn't shared with anyone, not even Rachelle that she'd met Russell Andrew Johnson, Bobby Addison Johnson's twin brother, and had been having ongoing conversations with him. She didn't know why she felt compelled to keep that promise Russell asked of her or why she felt some sense of loyalty to him, but she had. After all, she didn't even know the man. It wasn't like he was Bobby and she'd known him a while. She'd met Russell only weeks ago.

That night, Teyona and Steven lay in bed together; she was reading a case file while Steven leafed through a medical journal when his phone beeped alerting him to an incoming text. He checked the message, threw back the covers and hurriedly got out of bed.

"Where are you going?" Teyona asked, looking up from her file.

"I've got to get to the hospital. I'll call you from there, if I see that I'm going to be really late coming back home."

"Okay. Would you like me to make you a thermos of coffee?" Teyona asked, laying her file on the bed.

"No, I'm fine," he said, pulling on a pair of pants he took from the closet and a pullover from the drawer. He stuck his feet in his shoes, grabbed his keys and bag and left.

CHAPTER 19

RUSSELL

Russell parked several houses down the street from where Rachelle and George lived. He shut off the engine but left the radio on. Though he and Rachelle had worked together, he'd also been running surveillance on her almost from the time when he came to town. He watched her front door open as she exited, got into her car and drove away. Russell discreetly followed her directly to the Sheridan Hotel where she went inside and checked in. It wasn't long before Steven drove into the parking lot, got out of his car and entered the hotel and Russell took pictures of each of them entering the hotel and those pictures would have dates and time stamped on them.

Russell started his car and drove away. On the drive to his hotel, he made a call to Teyona. She answered, surprised to hear his voice. She asked, "How have you been? I haven't heard from you in a while."

"Does that mean you missed me?"

Teyona didn't respond to his comment, instead

she asked, "What can I do for you, Mr. Johnson?"

"You could stop calling me Mr. Johnson and call me Russell. That is my name, you know."

"Was there something that you wanted tonight, Mr. Johnson?"

"Don't get all professional on me. I thought we were becoming friends." He heard a deep sigh on the other end of the phone. He said, "I was out of town for a bit. Had some things I needed to check into. Can I see you tomorrow?"

"Do you think it's a good idea for us to keep seeing each other like this?"

"Yes, I do and I would appreciate it very much if you would please make a little time for me tomorrow. I really need to talk to you."

When Teyona looked at Russell or thought of him, she no longer saw Bobby Johnson. Yes, they had the same face, the same built; both tall and handsome. Yes, handsome. Very much so. Yet, they were different, so very different. Bobby with his playful personality and devil may care kind of attitude, was more like an overgrown boy who appealed to her youthful side, while Russell exuded sophistication, confidence and knowhow of a full grown man. Yes, Russell was the suave, more adult twin. "Can you come to my office after five tomorrow?" She asked.

"Why don't you come by my hotel?"

"I don't think that would be professional or appropriate," she said surprised that he would even suggest his hotel room for a meeting with her.

"You don't trust me, even if I promise to behave?"

"Be serious," she sniffed.

"I want to have a real conversation with you and share some things without interruptions, and I think if you come to me, we could accomplish that."

"I'm not sure I want to do that," she said, slowly. "I don't see a problem with you coming to my office and I believe we could achieve whatever you have in mind in my office so if you really want to talk with me, then I suggest you find your way over to my office after five tomorrow."

Russell sighed deeply. "Alright. I'll be there at five o one."

Teyona shook her head. "Tomorrow then. Goodnight, Mr. Johnson," she said, hung up and scooted down under the covers. She closed her eyes and tried to go to sleep but she wasn't successful. She found herself tossing and turning. Her mind filled with thoughts of Russell Johnson. What did he want to talk with her about now? She'd already told him everything she knew about his brother. There was really nothing else to talk about. She turned over in bed, punched the pillow and buried her face into it.

CHAPTER 20

RACHELLE

After Rachelle and Steven made love a second time, both completely sated, they lay in bed together and talked.

"We've got a problem," she announced, catching her breath.

"What kind of problem?" Steven blew out a huge breath and glanced over at her before returning his attention to the program that was on television.

"Momma is sick and she is unable to continue to take care of the baby."

That revelation caused Steven to sit up and turn his full attention to her. "Are you kidding me? What's going on with her?"

"She called tonight, told me she's not well and that she can no longer take care of the baby. That's what she said."

"I thought her neighbor was giving her a hand. What is it, do they want more money? I mean we can do that."

"Her neighbor had been coming in and helping out but neither of them is able to provide the appropriate care to a baby who isn't exactly an infant anymore."

"See," Steven began, wondering why she hadn't listened to him and had the abortion when she initially informed him she was pregnant. "I knew something like this was going to happen. I knew it." Steven threw his legs over the side of the bed and stood up. "This is definitely a problem, a fucking nightmare," he said, beginning to pace around the room. "What are you gonna do?"

His question caught Rachelle by surprise and made her angry. "What do you mean what am I gonna do? You're trying to dump all this shit on me? I didn't create this situation all by myself you know. We're in this shit together!"

"I didn't mean it like that," he lied, dropping back down on the bed, massaging his temples with both hands. He'd like nothing more than to leave Rachelle and her baby and never see either of them ever again.

"That's how it sounded to me."

Steven got up from the bed, and began to pace around the room again, running his hands back and forth over his head. "What'd wrong with your mother getting someone there to help with the baby. I don't see what the problem would be with that, do you?"

"I don't know if I want someone else raising our baby, Steven."

Steven dropped his hands and paced the room absentmindedly, "You should've ended the pregnancy when I told you to and we wouldn't be in this mess right now. That's the problem with you. You never listen. Always have to have it your way."

"I see where you're going with this but if you think you're gonna stick me with everything, don't even try it because if you do, I will fuck your life up. I mean it. Don't you play with me!" Rachelle's anger flared adding a threat to boot.

Steen turned to look at Rachelle. "What do you mean by that?" He asked, his fury matching hers.

"I'm just saying." She attempted to omit the part that sounded awfully like a threat.

Steven took a few steps toward Rachelle, "No, you tell me what the fuck you mean by what you just said? Are you threatening me?" His face was blood red and his voice was thunderous. "You're not trying to tell me that you might go to Teyona with this bull shit?"

"Oh, so this is bull shit to you now, huh? Is that how you see our son? As bull shit?" Rachelle tilted her head up, and her eyes grew soft. "I didn't realize how little you cared about Stevie Jr. I understand why you don't want him to live here with me but I thought it was to protect all the people involved. I didn't understand how you really feel about the baby."

"Have you given any thought about George and what this could do to your marriage?"

"Fuck George," she spat. "I don't care about what he might feel about our baby. I don't give a good damn about George. If I had it my way, our baby would've been born right here with you and me."

"You have lost your fucking mind. You are completely insane," he said and Rachelle could see veins popping up in his head.

"Don't you call me crazy. You're just trying to protect your reputation. You don't want your reputation tarnished. That's all this is about because you don't give a damn about anyone other than your little family." She stared at Steven a long time before she spoke again. "Why are you so damn protective of Teyona anyway? Do you think she'd be that protective of you?"

"Yes she would be."

"And you know that, how?"

"Look! I don't give a damn about none of this bullshit but leave Teyona out of it. I mean it, Rachelle! Do whatever you have to do to ensure that the boy is taken care of and I will handle all costs involved. Just don't you dare bring any embarrassment or problems to my damn door." Steven stopped to stare at Rachelle an instant before he said, shaking his head before dropping back down hard on the bed again and reclining, "What the hell have we gotten ourselves into?" he asked, looking up at the ceiling.

Rachelle ignored Steven's question. Instead she insisted, "Look, we just need to think about bringing Stevie Jr. here! That's all there is to it."

"I think we should talk about this some more, explore some other options," Steven offered.

Rachelle stood over Steven with one hand on her hip creating a surreal atmosphere almost like a mother admonishing her child. "Steven, we're out of options. You know the situation with mama. I've told you she's not well and can't take care of our child anymore and as far as I'm concerned, it's settled."

"The decision is not yours alone, Rachelle," Steven tried to appease her, returning to a sitting position on the bed. "We have to make a decision such as this together." He twisted his head from side to side, trying to remove the kink from his neck.

"Would you like me to give you a massage," Rachelle offered.

"No, I'm alright," he replied and returned to their previous conversation, "We'll work something out. Offer the neighbor a little extra money to take care of the baby until your mom recovers or something. Just give me a little time to think this through. We'll figure something out."

"I don't think mama's neighbor is gonna be receptive to that. After all, she's older than mama and her health isn't the best either."

"Have you talked with her or even asked if she could do it? I told you I'll be more than happy to take care of all the costs involved. She wouldn't have to worry about money. I just need a little time to figure some things out."

"It's not about the money, Steven. I think our child should be here, closer to both of his parents."

"Where's he going to live if you bring him here?"

Rachelle reclined on the bed, one hand propping up her head and giving Steven a sly smile. "I haven't decided what I'm gonna do yet but don't worry, if I decide to bring him here, he won't be living with me."

Steven frowned with concern. "There's something you're not telling me."

For years, Rachelle harbored a deep seated hatred for Teyona. She was angry with her not only because of her accomplishments but because of her looks, career and her husband. Rachelle had always been envious of Teyona and wanted that lifestyle for herself. Actually, she wanted Teyona's life. That was the reason she had gone out of her way to throw herself at Steven, seduce him and not only get pregnant after assuring him that she was on birth control, but to go as far as having his child. All of her actions were designed to hurt Teyona because she hated her so much. But she said to Steven, "I've told you everything that I know and that is I'm bringing our son here to live and that's the bottom line!"

Feeling his temper flare again, Steven grabbed his slacks from the floor, shoved his legs in and jerking them up, then pulled his sweater over his head.

"Where are you going so soon? You just got here. I was under the impression that you wanted to talk."

"What's left to talk about? It appears you've already made up your mind."

"That doesn't mean that we have to call it a night so soon. Why don't we hang out here another hour or so?"

"I'm going home." He jammed his feet into his shoes and got up from the bed. "I do have a wife who is there waiting for me. You know that, don't you?" He walked towards the door.

"I don't know how long that will last," Rachelle said under her breath before quickly realizing Steven heard enough of what she'd said to understand her meaning. He rushed back over, got on the bed where he was in Rachelle's face, menacing her as he gripped her arms.

"Bitch, I told you, not to fuck with me," he hurled at her. "You had better keep this shit away from my wife. Just because the pussy is good and I love it doesn't mean I'm gonna let you fuck me over. Do you understand me? You just keep this shit away from my wife. And, I don't want to have this conversation with you again."

Rachelle didn't respond, she just stared at Steven in disbelief. She'd always thought given the opportunity, Steven could fall in love with her. Sexually, she really turned him out and hadn't he already told his wife that if they weren't married that he'd be with her? She had to wonder whether what Steven felt for her was love or simply lust.

Steven arrived home, went upstairs and was surprised to find Teyona still awake. "How did it go at the hospital, honey?" she asked, sitting up in her side of the bed as he sat on the other side and kicked off his shoes.

"One of my patients is going to have to have surgery—kidney stones. He's in a lot of pain," he lied, stood up, and pulled his sweater over his head tossing it in the chair next to the bed. His pants landed on the chair beside it.

"Ooh, I'm sorry. I bet that is painful. Has the surgery been scheduled?"

"It is painful. He's been complaining about it for a while and I tried talking him into having the surgery weeks ago but he refused it, believing the pain would eventually go away."

"Patients can be so stubborn sometimes."

"Yeah, but we now have his surgery set for tomorrow night," Steven said, climbing into bed next to his wife.

"That's too bad he waited and endured the pain for so long but at least now he's made the decision and all be well soon." Teyona paused a moment. "Sounds like another long night for you, hon." She lay down, turned over in bed and snuggled up close to him. She saw distress all over his face. Steven cared about his patients as he did his family and he always tried to do what was best for them. He didn't appear to realize that he was only one person and couldn't solve everyone's problems. "It will be alright, baby," she said, not realizing how wrong she'd been about her husband. "I love you so much, Steven."

"I love you too, baby," Steven replied, with thoughts running rampant inside his head, none of which were pleasant and none involved any of his patients.

Soon afterwards, Teyona fell asleep; however, it was almost daylight before Steven closed his eyes and went off into troubled slumber.

CHAPTER 21

TEYONA & RACHELLE

Late that Sunday afternoon wearing an ultra sheer, cream colored, summer dress Rachelle got out of her car, walked up to the front door and pressed the doorbell at Teyona's house. "Damn," Teyona heard Rachelle say as she opened the door for her.

"What's wrong?" Teyona asked with concern as she stood back for Rachelle to enter.

"I broke a nail getting out of the car just now," Rachelle answered, annoyance on her face.

"Oh." The women embraced. When they released each other, Teyona noticed what her friend was wearing. She had called Rachelle out so many times about coming to her home inappropriately dressed but that didn't stop her. "What is that you are wearing?" Teyona shook her head. "I don't believe you're running the streets, commando no less, wearing a dress like that. What were you thinking leaving your house dressed like that?"

"Child, please. It's hot. How is a girl expected to keep cool?"

"Well, you should be plenty cool in what you're wearing. Girl, I can see everything you have, right down to that Brazilian wax," Teyona warned. "Come on in," she said, closing the door after Rachelle entered then brushing past her, walking down the hall towards the kitchen as Teyona made a quick dash upstairs.

Rachelle stopped to acknowledge Steven, who was sitting in a recliner in the den, with the newspaper in his lap while watching a game on TV. "Hello, Dr. Steven," she called out to him and waited patiently for him to look her way and get an eye full. "What's going on?"

"Rachelle." Steven glanced up and seeing how Rachelle was dressed, he added, "And, here you are. George let you out of the house like that?"

"As if George could do something about it," she retorted.

"All set for your trip?" Steven asked, looking down at the newspaper in his lap trying to avoid looking at everything Rachelle was dying for him to see.

"Damn right. Bahamas here we come. You guys are gonna miss out on a great trip."

"I understand several other girls are joining you and Teyona for this little adventure."

"Yeah, Charlotte, Tuesday and Avis are meeting us in Florida."

"Oh, Avis is going?" Steven asked in surprised since Avis had gotten married two weeks ago and had just returned from her honeymoon less than a week ago.

"Why? Avis can't go with us on this girls' trip because she's a newlywed?"

Steven lifted the newspaper from his lap and made a concerted effort to divert his eyes away from Rachelle. "You girls behave yourselves," he said dismissively to her, only Rachelle played to win and she had no intention of not getting Steven's full attention.

"Now, that would be no fun, would it?" she said with attitude and waited for a response, giving Steven a look, one that he returned in kind before she walked towards the kitchen with a sly grin on her face. She'd been carrying on an affair with him behind her best friend's back for several years and if she could trade places with Teyona, she'd do so in a skinny minute.

Rachelle lifted her phone from a pocket on her dress and dialed a number as she entered the kitchen where Teyona was standing, holding a brand new pair of panties in her hand.

"Here," Teyona said, tossing the panties to Rachelle. "Put these on."

Holding up the panties to examine them, Rachelle said, "What? These?"

"Yeah, those and they're brand spanking new, still got the tag on them. Put them on, Rachelle and don't come back to my house dressed like that again. I mean that. And remember, you are going to the nail salon after you leave here."

"These are granny panties,"

186

"They are not. You are just accustomed to wearing a postage stamp or nothing at all. Put them on and perhaps next time, you will wear something appropriate when you leave your house."

Rachelle looked at the panties again before the stepped into them. Then, looking at her phone, she said, "Nina? Sorry about that." She gave Teyona an eye for causing her to keep Nina waiting. "But can I get in this afternoon? I just broke a nail getting out the car and some friends and I are leaving in the morning for our Bahamas getaway so I need to get a fix today, girl. Can you help a sista out?" she asked and waited for a response. She looked at her watch. "Let's see. It is now three fifteen. Okay, four thirty is fine. I'll see you than. You're the best, Nina. Thanks, girl." Rachelle ended the call as she went over and took a seat at the island.

"You and George weren't at church today," Teyona said. "Everything's alright?"

"Yeah, things are fine. I was up quite late last night packing for our trip and this morning I was tired as hell, so we decided to just stay in and rest."

"We missed you both," Teyona said and asked, "so you're about finished packing?"

"I have to add a couple of things but for the most part, I'm pretty much done."

"Before I leave, I want to see the swimsuits you're taking."

"Okay. Last week, I went back to that neat little swimwear shop and bought that one piece sunburst suit that we were looking at."

"Oh, at Evelyn's Swimwear. That is a neat little shop."

"Yeah. I got that one, another white one piece and a black two piece that is really cute."

Rachelle's fingers were busy responding to a text message. It was Steven. His message read, *'Go home and put some clothes on your naked ass.'* Her response was, *'Why don't you come and make me, lover.'* Then, with a devious smile on her face, she placed her phone down on the counter top. "Sounds scrumptious," she said to Teyona. "I packed three also. The lime green suit is one to die for and I can't wait to see myself on the beach, under that gorgeous sun in that one. I'm taking a black one also and one is in a tropical print. Girl, I just want to blend right in." She grinned.

"Speaking of scrumptious, I made a pie." Teyona turned and went over to take the pie from atop the stove, put it on the island counter and began to slice it. "You want a piece?" she asked, and without waiting for an answer, she went off to get saucers from the cabinet above the sink and a couple of forks from the drawer. "How is George?"

"What kind of pie is that?"

"Sweet potato."

"Yeah, I'll definitely have some sweet potato pie. That's my favorite."

"I know."

"From the way they look, I can't tell a sweet potato pie from the pumpkin. You love pumpkin pie but you know how I feel about it. I am so not a fan," Rachelle said, grinning, then answered

Teyona's previous question, "But back to George, George is George. He's fine." She shrugged. "You got coffee?"

"I just put on a pot a while ago. I was happy when you told me last night that things are a little better between you and George. As long as it is progressing in the right direction, that's a positive." Then Teyona called out to Steven, "Honey, would you like a piece of pie and some coffee?"

"I'll have some later, babe," he replied.

"Okay," she answered him, then she said to Rachelle, "As I've always said, George is a great guy and if you throw him out there, some thirsty woman is gonna snatch his butt up in a New York Minute. Most women are looking for a good man and as we both know, George is an exceptional man."

"I know. Those THOTS are standing in line."

"You're so crazy," Teyona said and they laughed.

Before Teyona could put slices of pie on the saucers, Rachelle had picked up a fork and began eating the pie from its pan.

"Seriously, no one is throwing anyone away." Rachelle cut off a piece of pie and put it into her mouth. "I suppose George and I hit a rough patch but we're trying to work through it."

"That's great. A lot of couples encounter problems in their marriage one time or another. I'm just glad that you guys didn't give up on each other and are giving it another chance. You had me worried there for a minute." Then, grinning,

Teyona grabbing two cups, placing them on a tray with cream and sweetner. She filled the cups with coffee and setting them on the island counter top, she asked, "How are things in the bedroom?"

Rachelle grinned also as she forked another piece of pie into her mouth. "Well, George has always been good in bed, but unlike your husband, he's no core shaker," she said.

"What?" Teyona laughed and Rachelle joined in. When the laughter stopped, Teyona asked, "Are you excited about the trip?"

"Yes I am. A little sun and fun away from work will do us all good. Just what the doctor ordered," Rachelle said, she and Teyona looked at each other and laughed at their inside joke as Rachelle forked more pie into her mouth and sipped more coffee from her cup.

"I definitely agree with that." Sitting and enjoying a moment with Rachelle like this, Teyona wished she hadn't promised Russell she wouldn't share that they'd met. She felt she was betraying her best friend. Only, she had no way of knowing that Rachelle was not the friend she'd thought she was, and her comparing George's bedroom skills to Steven was true because unbeknown to Teyona, Rachelle knew all about Steven's sexual skills.

Teyona didn't notice the malevolent look Rachelle gave her before she smiled to herself over her coffee cup. She couldn't wait to wipe that smug, satisfied look off of Teyona's face. And that day would surely come and not soon enough.

"Have you gotten any more pictures?" Rachelle asked and watched as Teyona's face darkened.

"No, I haven't."

"That was just crazy. I will never understand what that was about," Rachelle lied, knowing full well that she was as much to blame as Russell about those pictures Teyona received.

"Neither will I. I just hope whoever was doing that to me, will stop it," she sighed deeply as she picked up a fork and leaning across the counter, she joined Rachelle as they ate sweet potato pie and drank coffee together.

Shortly after five that Monday afternoon under clear, blue skies, Teyona, Rachelle, Avis, Tuesday and Charlotte landed in the Bahamas. After checking for their five star accommodations at the Casa Del Mario Hotel, they took the elevator to their five bedroom suite. They entered the suite and the women let out lots of ooohs and ahhhs as they were greeted by a beautiful array of colors from the accent pieces, couches, chairs and pillows all made from lively, vibrant floral fabrics and some solids to white wicker tables, chrome and porcelain lamps, palm plants throughout the suite and a view that was nothing short of breathtaking.

"Oh gee, isn't this gorgeous," Rachelle said, admiring the open spacious layout of their suite.

"Yeah, girl. This place is so fabulous," Teyona said, complimenting Rachelle on such a beautiful find.

"Oh my," Avis, the youngest and most recently married one of the group, agreed. "This is gonna be such fun."

"Count on it," Rachelle said, grinning.

"Look at Rachelle. Doesn't she always look like she has an agenda, y'all," Charlotte commented.

"You noticed that too?" Teyona said, laughing before adding, "Will you just look at that view." She gazed out across the ocean. "This is gorgeous."

"Now, this is escapism, pure paradise. I could get lost right here," Rachelle said.

"You can say that again. It is breathtaking," Avis said, enjoying the spectacular view.

"Yes it is. Absolutely awesome," Tuesday said as she looked out beyond the terrace to the rippling waters of the ocean.

"Get a look at that ocean," Charlotte said. "Heavenly. Come on girls. Let's get out of these clothes into some skimpy swimwear, hit the beach and mix with the natives."

"Yeah, let's get this party started," Tuesday said, laughing and breaking into one of her dance moves.

"I'm with you," Rachelle said, dancing to her own imaginary music.

Rachelle, I have to admit," Teyona began, looking out across the ocean. "This is one of your better ideas, girl. I'm realizing now how much I really needed this."

Bowing at the waist, Rachelle said, "At your service, ma'am."

All the women chuckled.

The suite was an open floor plan, the living space leading directly into a full dining room, kitchen, stopping at the terrace, overlooking the ocean with its breathtakingly blue-green, sparkling and beautiful waters.

"This is gonna be so good. Rachelle, you really outdid yourself, hooking us up in this great place," Teyona said.

"I aim to please, ladies," Rachelle responded. "Select your room, get changed and we can begin to do what we do best. Remember, we're here for only three days. So let's make the most of our time."

Selecting a room they deposited their bags, replaced their clothes with swim suits and went down to the beach for some fun in the sun, encountering happy, sexy people. Some of the young women were running around wearing postage stamp size swim suits and enjoying the sun, beach, the ocean and attention.

Teyona and her friends spent the rest of the afternoon walking along the beach, talking and giggling hysterically while kicking their toes in the white powdery sand and collecting seashells or splashing in the ocean. While having fun on the beach, the women ran into several guys who talked them into joining them at one of the local nightclubs that evening.

After dressing in their sexiest outfits that evening, the women took a cab to their destination. Upon entering Club Oasis, they were met immediately by the three island men they spoke with on the beach earlier that day as well as two additional men. After some joyful, mindless chatter and fine dining, they had tasty drinks with fruit and umbrellas, giggled a lot, watching the sexy and ratchet dancing going on, on the dance floor. Although Teyona and the others noticed Rachelle getting a little too cozy with one of the men with them, Teyona was also reminded that the recently widowed neurosurgeon who danced with her most of the evening, had displayed a more than casual interest in her until she assured him she was happily married and had no interest in changing anything about that. Apparently, Rachelle had not been so forthcoming.

At the end of the evening, the men accompanied the ladies back to their hotel and after saying good night, the ladies went up to their suite. After changing into their sleepwear and gathered comfortably, the women lounged in the living area, chatting and listening to the sound of the ocean through the open terrace doors.

"This is just what I needed," Teyona said, relaxing in a chaise.

"How did the rest of you ladies enjoyed your first day here?" Rachelle asked, going over to the mini bar to make herself a drink.

"Great," Charlotte said and asked, "Did you all see how the guy, I believe Matthew was his name, was trying to get all up on me at the club tonight?"

"You believe his name was Matthew, huh," Rachelle teased, giggling, carrying a drink in her hand and sat. "Yeah, right."

"Un huh, I saw that," Tuesday grinned, in response to Charlotte.

"You only brought a drink for yourself?" Avis said, laughing.

"That's how Rachelle rolls," Tuesday said, giving Rachelle a dark eye before going over to the bar and returned with a tray of drinks that she offered each girl.

"Matthew is one fine brotha too," Avis said.

"Look who's talking," Charlotte said, directing her comment at Avis. "Derek has got your nose so wide open that I didn't think you noticed other men."

The woman chuckled.

Avis raised a finger. "I'm in love with my husband but that isn't to say that I am blinded to other attractive men. I wouldn't cross the line but I'm definitely gonna look when I see something fine to look at and those men were fine—all of them." She chuckled.

"I heard that, Avis," Tuesday leaned over and gave her the high five.

"We're all here to have a great time," Rachelle said. "Let's just loosen up and have fun. We don't have to take ourselves so seriously all the time, y'all, damn. Shake it up a little."

"Yes, mother," Tuesday said, giggling.

"I know you've had too much to drink now if you're calling me mother," Rachelle responded, laughing.

"So what are we doing tomorrow? Any one has anything special in mind or should we just play it by ear, be spontaneous?" Teyona asked.

"Let's just play it by ear and whatever comes up, we will do it," Charlotte said.

"Sound good to me, Teyona said.

Talking a while longer before ending their conversation, they said good night and went off to rooms.

Teyona's room was between Avis and Rachelle's. Sometime during the night, Teyona got up and went to the bathroom. While there, she thought she heard voices coming from Rachelle's room. She initially thought some of the girls had gotten together in Rachelle's room for a late night snack or just more girls' talk. As she was about to leave the bathroom to return to her room, she heard voices again and one of those voices sounded like a male. She listened. Nothing, it became quiet. As Teyona was again about to leave the bathroom, she heard the voices again; low, muffled sounds before they grew increasingly louder, drifting through the door. One was Rachelle's, the other was definitely a man's voice with a rich island accent and from the sounds coming from the room, they were having sex. Rachelle didn't know anyone on the island but there she was, having wild, loud sex with someone, a man, a man she didn't even know, Teyona thought, incredulously. Rachelle was in bed, having sex with a complete stranger. Teyona's stomach curled at the unpleasant thought. How could Rachelle do that? She wondered. She knew that people do change, but the old Rachelle would never do something like that. When had she changed so drastically? By leading this double life, she'd definitely broken her vows of being honest. Her honor code was shattered.

Teyona went back to bed and tossed and turned, trying to go back to sleep but sleep was not forthcoming. She knew Rachelle had cheated on George once years ago, but they'd worked through those issues. Recently when they experienced another small bump in the road, she thought they'd resolved that. Obviously, that hadn't happened.

The next morning, the women got up, spent some time on the terrace, enjoying the ocean along with cups of coffee they made from the hotel's complimentary samples in their suite and they talked. Later, they changed into beachwear and enjoyed a late breakfast at their hotel's extravagant buffet consisting of toast, biscuits, scrambled eggs, bacon, ham, sausage, fried plantain, mixed fruit, cereal, milk, juice, coffee and hot chocolate. Rachelle was especially bubbly, chattering nonstop as she smothered jelly on her biscuit that she began eating heartily. Teyona didn't mention to her what she'd heard coming from her room the night before, but from the way Rachelle kept trying to give her hidden looks, Teyona felt Rachelle was aware that she knew.

After breakfast and donning fashionable and provocative swim suits, the ladies went out and found chairs near the hotel pool, where they ordered shots, requested that wine be brought out later, and engaged in lively conversation.

"That was a wonderful article in Black Enterprises this month, Teyona," Charlotte said. "Great cover too. I'm so proud of you and Steven. You guys are really doing the damn thing."

"Thank you, Charlotte. We were excited when they called to do our story and for us to do their cover," Teyona said with pride, then asked, "How is Yasmine?"

"Yasmine is doing just fine with her grown self," Charlotte said, laughing. "She has been grown from the day she was born."

"She still wants to be a doctor?" Avis inquired.

"Yeah, girl," Charlotte answered. "Since she was about seven years old. Yasmine will be going into her sophomore year in college this fall."

"She's at Emory University, right?" Avis asked.

"Yeah," Charlotte replied.

"That is terrific," Tuesday said. "You must be so proud of her especially for keeping her head on straight. Apparently she knew what she wanted early on and has remained focused all this time."

Charlotte said, "Yes, I am very proud of her."

"Tuesday, how is that old fine ass man of yours," Rachelle asked, just as their shots arrived, carried by a handsome, well build native with a huge white toothed smile. "Hello handsome," she greeted him."

"Hello, Madam," the server replied.

"I'm Rachelle. Madam is my mother," she said and the girls chuckled. "You got a woman here on the island?"

"Rachelle," Avis said, laughing.

"Mind your business, Chile, I'm trying to get myself fixed up here," Rachelle said to Avis and the ladies chuckled again.

"Are you forgetting that you are a married woman?" Tuesday gave her a sly look.

"I believe I'm capable of handling my own affairs, and news flash, I'm not forgetting anything nor am I gonna ask this fine brotha to marry me, but I am gonna ask him if he's involved with someone, which more than likely he is, but if he is, does he date outside his relationship. I certainly could teach him a thing or two." Rachelle gave the server a sexy look, adding, "His mind, body and soul."

"She's just having fun with you, young man," Teyona said.

The server smiled as he placed the tray with the shots on the table nearest them and left, smiling again over his shoulder at Rachelle. She reciprocated.

"Aren't you already married?" Charlotte repeated almost the same question as Tuesday.

"Charlotte, where have you been? Didn't you just ask the same question as Tuesday?" Avis questioned, laughing. "I want to say you've had too much to drink but you haven't had anything stronger than coffee to drink this morning."

"Yeah, Charlotte," Tuesday laughed, "If you're that far out there already, I think you'd better leave the bottle alone and the dating to us single women."

Avis said, directing her comment to Rachelle, "That's right, Rachelle because what you're talking about doing is not a good look. Seriously."

"Bye, Felicia," Rachelle said, sarcastically with a wave of her hand. "Hell, we're here to have some fun and you're either with it or you are not, but in any event, don't try to rain on my damn parade." She shrugged and added with a giggle, "Besides, I'm so cool with my shit that by the time George catches up to what I *had* been doing, I would have already moved on. Girls, you gotta be smart. You gotta out think 'em."

"You just can't keep those knees together, can you?" Avis asked, giving Rachelle a sly smile.

"Oh man, do I have to?" Rachelle came back, throwing back her shot and setting the glass back on the table. "Look girls, I'm hot, I can't help it that all the boys love me and want to get with this." She smiled, patting the triangle between her thighs. "It happens, alright. Deal with it." She shrugged her bare shoulders. "I'm just saying."

Charlotte giggled.

Teyona giggled, "Girl you're so crazy."

"Yeah, crazy like a fox." Rachelle reclined on her chaise. "You girls call me crazy. I call it being sexually free. Besides, regardless to what I do, George is always gonna want me. Even when I piss him off, all I gotta do is put that dick in my mouth and clamp my teeth down on it." She flipped her hands in the air. "He is through and I get to have and do whatever the hell I want."

200

"For what it's worth," Teyona chimed in, grinning, "That young man certainly is a walking wet dream, if I must say so myself."

"See. Out of the mouth of the therapist herself," Rachelle said, giggling.

"The therapist wasn't suggestion you do anything other than admire at a distance." Teyona sipped from her drink glass.

"Still, I say don't let these powder blue skies, crystal waters and white sand beach cause you to throw away all your normal good sense," Tuesday interjected. "With a man like George, you get to check all the boxes. He's a good man, handsome, tall, well built, brown skinned, well educated brotha with his own business and who offers that extra bonus of knowing how to sling it in the bedroom."

"Amen," Avis said.

"Not to mention that he's hopelessly in love with that woman," Teyona shared.

"What are you all doing, writing his resume?" Rachelle retorted.

Tuesday said, "No, nothing like that. I'm just saying George is the man."

"I understand you wanting to have a great time here on this beautiful island but seriously, what would George say if he knew you were running around here with those kinds of thoughts in that mind of yours?" Avis asked.

"Although I don't owe you heffas a damn thing, I did the decent thing and told all of you my position, but for future reference, Hash Tag, '*what*

George doesn't know surely won't hurt him,' will it?" Rachelle said, grinning.

"I'm clutching my pearls, honey," Charlotte said, her hand went to her chest as she and Tuesday squealed with laughter, giving each other a high five.

The server returned with a tray of drinks and an extra bottle of wine that he set on the table. Before he left, he flashed Rachelle another bright smile that wasn't missed by anyone, especially Rachelle. She looked at the ladies and all their eyes were turned on her. She said, "Don't hate me cause you ain't me." She waved a hand in the air. "I'm not the kind of gal who waits for things to happen, I make them happen." She looked at the girls. "I'm just keeping it one hundred. How about that?" Then, she directed her next comment to Avis. "You are a young, sexy gal, I don't know what harm it would be if you got your feet wet with a couple of these island boys."

Avis smiled, shaking her head. "No thank you very much but I'm not that girl."

"To each her own," Rachelle said.

Each woman took a glass. "We have to make a toast," Teyona said, her glass raised.

"I'm toasting to us getting laid by some of these fine young bucks. I hear they have some kind of rhythm going on and can go all night long," Rachelle said and they roared with laughter as they clicked their glasses.

After a while, they rubbed sunscreen lotion over their bodies and basked in the sun. Later, they swam in the ocean, even later, returned to the hotel, got dressed and went shopping at some of the island stores for souvenirs. Sometime later, they returned to the hotel with each woman going off to her room laden with purchases.

Early evening, the ladies ate a leisurely meal. Teyona, Rachelle and Avis, talked about their husbands, work, antique shopping, and books, while Charlotte and Tuesday, both divorced, talked about their careers, men they were dating, men they wanted to date and movies. Later that evening, they left the hotel and went to a different nightclub someone on the beach mentioned to them. The Balboa Cove had lots of sexual activities happening on the wall-mounted projection screens but they got their fill sipping lots of great drinks and dancing for hours to lively island music.

On the way back to the hotel, they came across a concert on the beach. A small stage erected in the sand near the ocean and a three-piece band at the back of the stage played lively tunes accompanying a young woman out front with a really nice voice, belting out a combination of popular American songs and some island favorites. The women swayed back and forth together, listening to the music, dancing, enjoying the breezes and the sound of the ocean as the waves rolled in and out. Before long, they'd removed their shoes and walked along the edge of the ocean with the ocean slapping around their ankles.

When they returned to the hotel that evening, they had drinks and chatted some more.

"I heard that someone got in a little extra circular activity last night," Charlotte snickered and rolled her eyes towards the ceiling. "I'm not saying who it was but I am saying it should have been me. I'm jealous," she giggled.

"Really? Who?" Tuesday asked but she had already heard that it was Rachelle who'd had a guest in her room last night after they all had gone to bed.

"I'm not saying, but that's what I heard," Charlotte said, as they ladies looked at each other and chuckling, they pointed towards one another.

"I heard some wild noises coming from somebody's room last night also," Avis chimed in, smiling, a knowing look on her face.

"Y'all go to hell," Rachelle jumped in saying. "I don't know what's the big deal if someone got a little action while here on this gorgeous, tropical, island. We're all grown ass women and we're free to do as we damn well please. I wouldn't hold it against any of you for getting some." Rachelle shrugged her shoulders nonchalantly. "As far as I am concerned, I'm gonna live, I'm gonna love, and I'm gonna enjoy and I don't need anyone's permission. I assume that holds true for the rest of you bitches also."

"So you were the lucky one," Charlotte said.

"Oh no, I'm not saying that. I'm just saying that I would if I wanted to," Rachelle insisted. "I wish it had been me. Hell, it should have been me. I'm raw, I'm real and I'm relentless when it comes to going after what I want, but unfortunately, it wasn't

204

me." When she looked up, she and Teyona eyes briefly met until Rachelle smiled furtively and looked away

"Whatever," Tuesday said, throwing her hands in the air. "You know what they say. What happens in the Bahamas stays in the Bahamas, right?"

Rachelle was in full agreement. "I heard that," she said, giving Tuesday the thumbs up.

The ladies chuckled and continued sipping their wine.

It wasn't long before Rachelle said good night and went off to her room. A short time later *Lady Sings the Blues*, an old classic movie which Diana Ross and Billy Dee Williams starred in that had Charlotte and Tuesday swooning over Billy Dee, went off, the others went to their rooms.

Sometime during the night, Teyona lifted her phone from the night table and checked the time. Three forty-five in the morning. If Rachelle had a man in her room, surely, he'd be gone by now, she thought. The bathroom was located between her and Rachelle's room and she didn't want to run the risk of running into a stranger there. Teyona threw back the covers, got out of bed and headed to the bathroom. She gently knocked on the door. Since it appeared no one was in there, she entered, closed the door and then from Rachelle's room, she was shocked to hear noises again, sexual noises. There was no mistaking it. Rachelle had invited some random lover into her room again. And, from the sound of the man's voice, he was not from the island which means Rachelle had slept with two different strange men in the span of two days. What was she thinking? Teyona wondered. Before returning to bed, Teyona filled a glass with water from the faucet over the sink, drank most of it and after locking the door between the bathroom and her bedroom, she returned to bed.

After spending three gloriously relaxing and wonderful days on the island, the ladies boarded the plane to return to the States. They were seated with their seat belts fastened and the pilot made his announcements over the address system, Teyona, sitting in a window seat, turned to Rachelle and asked, "Is there something you want to share with me?"

Rachelle looked at Teyona and replied innocently, "No, I don't think so. Why? What are you talking about?"

Teyona took several deep breaths, wondering why Rachelle was pretending she didn't know what she was talking about. She gave Rachelle a sad look. "Really?" She said, knowing Rachelle was not telling her the truth. "Don't play innocent with me, Rachelle. You and I are friends, have been for a long time and we know each other inside and out. I know what I heard, you know what you did and you know exactly what I'm talking about. I thought you and George were trying to work things out."

"I have no idea what you're talking about."

"Sure you do."

"No I don't"

"Are you kidding me right now?" she asked, her eyebrows arched. "You can't be serious, Rachelle.

206

Are you saying you were not having sex with some guy in your room the first night we arrived on the island and again last night?" She kept her voice low so that no one else would hear their conversation.

"No, I wasn't. I don't even know anyone on the island. Where would you get such an idea?"

"I heard you, Rachelle."

"What were you doing, eavesdropping at the door?"

"No, I wasn't eavesdropping at the door. I got up to use the bathroom and I distinctly heard your voice and that of a man, both nights, coming from your room and each night, it sounded like you two were really going at it."

"Oooh, tell me more," Rachelle said laughing off Teyona's allegations. "I could get off on a conversation like this."

"Don't, Rachelle. Don't."

"Why don't you stay in your own lane and mind your own damn business," Rachelle said harshly.

Surprised by her tone, Teyona said, "Rachelle, wow."

"Seriously, you don't see me all up in your business. Why can't you stay out of mine?"

"I didn't mention what I heard to upset you and frankly, I am surprised at your attitude. What's going on with you anyway? It's like I don't even know you anymore." Teyona resigned herself to the fact that Rachelle didn't want to share with her what she'd done while on the island. "You are a grown woman and you are free to do as you please so if you don't want to talk with me about what you and

I both know you were doing, then that is your right."

"You're not gonna make me admit to doing something I didn't do."

Teyona just looked at her friend.

"And. Don't judge me when you don't know the facts."

"I'm not judging you."

"Yes you are. I see it in your eyes," Rachelle said, lifted her nose in the air and looked away with a devious smile on her face.

Teyona blinked. She knew what she heard and she knew her friend was lying to her. She also knew that for the past several months, Rachelle had been acting strangely and she didn't know what to make of it. But, there was no reason to pursue the conversation further since Rachelle had flatly denied the allegations and made Teyona feel like a complete fool.

Rachelle turned to look out the window and saw that Teyona was still looking at her. She huffed annoyingly and asked indignantly, "Are you about ready to drop this or do you want to continue to run this conversation into the ground?"

Teyona took a deep, calming breath. "No, let's forget it. I'm done with it."

The two women continued to look at each other a moment longer, then Teyona shook her head and turned to look out the window. Suddenly, something occurred to her. She and Russell had met and talked almost a dozen times since they initially met and they were getting to know each other better. She was beginning to open up more to him, trust him and she believed he was beginning to trust her. She noticed each time she mentioned Rachelle, Russell would ask for assurance that she not mention that they'd met. What was that about? Was Russell trying to tell her something or protect her from someone? Her gut feeling was that she was missing something. Something very important.

When the women returned home, Teyona never brought up the subject of Rachelle having sex with strangers while on the island and neither did she.

CHAPTER 22

RUSSELL & TEYONA

Russell had been busy. Continuing with his investigation of the remaining players involved with his brother's death, he was now ready to approach Teyona with what he'd learned. He called her at her office late Thursday afternoon and asked to see her. It took some cajoling on Russell's part especially when he told her where he wanted to meet up with her at and at what time, but she agreed.

Teyona worked late Friday, seeing additional patients and reviewing patients' treatment plans. Although still early in her treatment program, her patient who was a cutter, was showing some signs of improvements. Teyona felt sure that should she continue to follow the program outlined for her and surround herself with positive people and situations, that she would one day overcome that issue. Before her appointed meet up time with Russell, she went home for a change of clothes. She dressed in jeans, blazer and sneakers before meeting up with him in a well lit downtown parking garage.

While waiting for Teyona, Russell gave a once over on the evidence he collected. He had gathered tons of damning pictures and videos to prove his case. His heart went out to Teyona. She was such a warm, kind, loving and trusting soul. He knew she would have difficulty seeing his materials. Tons of lies were going to be exposed tonight. He feared maybe she couldn't handle it. In the midst of his musing, he saw the headlights of a car approaching. He quickly gathered all his materials and slipped them in the large envelope before placing the envelope in the car pocket.

Teyona parked her car besides Russell, set her car alarm, got into his car and they drove away. They rode in silence. From time to time, Teyona glanced over at Russell, wondering what he was up to, what did he want to see her about this time, did he want to talk more about his brother?

Russell drove at least ten minutes before he pulled into the parking lot next to Steven's office building. "Why are we here?" she asked, breaking the silence and looking around the parking lot before returning her gaze to his face.

He chose not to answer her question. He switched off the car radio and for a moment, they sat in silence. When he spoke, he said, "I know what I'm about to say to you isn't appropriate. As a matter of fact, it is totally inappropriate and unprofessional on so many levels, but I have to say it anyway and let the chips fall where they may." Her body rigid, Teyona gazed at him, confusion covering her face. Russell continued, "I see why my brother fell so completely in love with you." Teyona gasped, her mouth wide open as she stared at Russell. She was taken aback, absolutely stunned by his comment. "It is so clear now."

She could've told him it was a mistake, her getting into his car and coming there in the first place, but she didn't. Instead she said, "I don't know what you mean."

"When I first saw you, I thought the reason my brother fell in love with you was because of your incredible good looks because you're gorgeous. The way you look would attract any man if he's got a heartbeat." Russell smiled.

Teyona began to feel uncomfortable. She lifted her eyes, tilted her head and studied him thoughtfully.

"You don't have to be afraid of me," Russell responded to her unspoken concerns. "I would never hurt you, and if you will permit me, I would never let anyone ever hurt you again. You've been through enough."

She didn't know what to say, she was at a loss for words. What did he know about her, her life and the people in her life?

"When I came to town, I came with vengeance in my mind, in my heart. I was gonna hurt everyone who hurt me by hurting my brother. Especially you." He looked at her, his eyes holding hers. "I wanted to hurt you most. I came here thinking you were this rich, entitled, high class bitch who went after a younger man to get your kicks for as long as it pleased you and when you got tired of him, you

212

threw him away like a piece of trash. He fought back and got himself killed in the process." He paused and looked out towards the medical building before he spoke again. "After meeting you and getting to know you, I learned a lot about you. You are so completely different than what I initially thought and I am happy to say that I was wrong about you." A frown crossed Russell's handsome face as he glanced at Teyona again before returning his attention back in the direction of the building that he was holding watch on. "Yep, my intentions were to hurt you; mentally at first, emotionally, then physically."

Teyona wasn't shocked or even surprised by what Russell was telling her. She had picked up some of what he was saying now in some of their previous conversations but she'd believed he had the right to feel the way he did and she wanted to be accommodating. "I know now that you aren't one hundred percent to blame for what happened to my brother. I can even see how this all came about. I've gotten to know that husband of yours and I completely understand how you got involved with Bobby. You were neglected. You spent a lot of time alone when it shouldn't have been that way. He was off doing his thing, leaving you to fend for yourself. That wasn't right. It also wasn't right what happened between you and Bobby, but your old man deserved that and so much more," he said and Teyona wondered what in the world he was talking about. What had Steven done other than be the exceptional doctor that he was, an excellent father and a truly loving and devoted husband.

"If I were married to a woman like you," Russell said breaking into her reverie, "I would be at home with her about as much as I would be at work." He laughed to himself. "I could never neglect someone like you. It's only been months but as I said, I feel that I've gotten to know you somewhat and there's some strange connection going on between us. You may never admit it, but there is some attraction going on with you and me." Russell paused a moment. Teyona remained silent. "I know now that you would've done anything not to hurt Bobby. I can see that it was a life or death situation for you and *that husband of yours*," Russell uttered the words with such distaste that Teyona wondered why he had such animosity towards her husband. "I've looked into the lives of your family, some of your friends and I believe I have everything I need. You have suffered the most in this situation but you are the most innocent." He ran a hand down over his face. "I've been wrong about you, so wrong and one day I'm gonna ask you to forgive me for what I've done to you. I would ask you to right now but that would be too soon because there is still so much that you have to process, but I will one day. . .soon. I'm not going to dismiss things that I've done to cause you stress but that won't happen again, ever. The pictures." He turned and looked at Teyona. He could tell what she was thinking and she was right. "Yes," he said, "I'm responsible for those pictures you'd been getting, but I had help with that."

Teyona finally broke her long silence. "Someone was helping you to hurt me?"

"Yes."

"Someone got into my home, took pictures and gave them to you," Teyona said; it was a statement, not a question. "The pictures were either doctored or you were in the pictures to make me think it was Bobby?"

"There was a lot of trick photography going on in those pictures but I've got others pictures that are one hundred percent authentic. Think about it. It had to be someone close to you, someone you know, someone who has been in your home. How else would I have gotten images of the inside of your home?"

Teyona had a number of friends who'd been in their new home. When they moved initially, family and friends were stopping by all the time so it was difficult to even guess who would've done something so conniving to her.

"I was able to get those images, superimposed my own image with them and what did you think you had? Bobby resurrected from the dead back to get you."

Shaking slightly, Teyona forced herself to look away from him and blew out a deep breath. She had so many questions. Would she ever get answers?

"You're an incredible woman. You're gorgeous, smart. You have got my heart doing summersaults and I can't control it."

Initially there was a sharp intake of breath but recovering quickly, she gave a tiny shrug, trying to affect an air of indifference before saying, "I wish you wouldn't talk to me like that. I am a married woman and I really don't want to listen to you tell me how you feel about me. I really don't." She took another deep breath and asked, "Are you going to tell me why you seem to hate my husband so much and who helped you to hurt me?" Then, recalling during the past several months she'd gotten to know Russell well also and she knew enough to not ask questions about anything he wasn't ready to share. He would answer all questions in his own time. "As a matter of fact, I'd really like you to take me back to my car."

"I want you to see something first."

"What is it? What could you possible want me to see?"

"Just be patient. You'll see," he said, then added, "You know, some of us search for something different, something unforgettable but when we find it, more often than not, we don't know what the hell to do with it. Have you found that to be true?"

It took Teyona a moment to respond. "Yes," she answered truthfully.

"I know you feel you betrayed your husband, and you move from day to day wallowing in guilt for getting involved with my brother. I know you do. I see it all over you. Your husband doesn't deserve you feeling all that guilt. As a matter of face, he doesn't deserve you. *Your husband* is a lying ass, son of a bitch."

Teyona wasn't going to sit there and allow this man to verbally destroy her husband. What could he possibly know about Steven that would cause him to say those harsh words? Could it be that he was upset with Steven for neglecting her, resulting in her getting involved with Bobby and him ultimately getting killed? Was that it? Teyona had dealt with many of her patients who had assigned blame to one person for what an entirely different person had done. Still, she had no problem defending her husband. "Why are you saying those horrible things about my husband when you don't even know him?"

"You think I don't? I beg to differ."

Teyona's mind had not been sharp since before she shot Bobby Johnson. All of that and the recently received pictures had clouded her thoughts, her judgment. Situations that she'd previously handled with enormous ease had become more difficult as time went by. Had she gone back to work too soon, before allowing herself to completely heal? Not allowing time to go through the necessary process, returning to involve herself in stressed related situations too soon, resulting in her slow reaction to situation, not being able to wrap her mind around a problem, assess it and solve it?

"Do you think your husband would cheat on you and if he did, do you think he'd feel guilty?"

Teyona was stunned by those questions. She raised her chin, looked him in his eyes and defiantly replied, "My husband would never cheat on me."

"Are you sure about that?"

"I didn't finish answering your questions. But as I was saying, one;" she enumerated with a finger,

"No, my husband would never cheat on me, and two, if something occurred in our marriage that would cause him to cheat, then yes, he would feel guilt for what he'd done."

"You don't know your husband very well, do you?"

"I absolutely do know my husband," she continued to defend Steven. "My husband loves me unconditionally. Unlike myself, he wouldn't betray me as I did him. He just wouldn't hurt me like that."

"Love you?" Russell paused before continuing, "Yes, I believe he does love you. How could he not love you? But, your husband is capable of a lot more than you might think," he said then asked, "Just in this past week alone, how often has he been late coming home?"

"I don't know what you're getting at? Besides, that's none of your business."

"That man is a flesh and blood man. He's just as human as you and I so don't give him too much credit. You will suffer a lot of heartbreak, if you do."

"It appears that you're the only one who's trying to hurt me right now."

That comment stung. The last thing Russell wanted to do was hurt Teyona. And although he'd promised her he'd make sure no one ever hurt her again, what he had to show her would take her far beyond any past pain she'd ever experienced, but he hoped he'd be around to help her get through the hurt. Later, if she'd allow him, he'd help her through all the pain she'd been through this past year, especially these past months. "Have you ever thought of surprising your husband at his office some night when he's working late?"

Before Teyona could respond, a sleek dark Lexus rolled into the parking lot, stopping near the door at Steven's office building. She and Russell watched as Rachelle got out of her car, dressed to kill and walked through the door that Steven was holding open for her.

"What do you think about that?" Russell asked.

"That's Rachelle. Steven is her physician and she sometime goes to see him after hours."

"Dressed to the nines, huh? Don't know the last time I've seen a patient go in to see her doctor dressed like that," he said, sarcastically. "And you don't have a problem with that?"

"Why would I?" she asked and stated, "If this is why you brought me here, we can leave now."

"You can give your husband and best friend all the benefit of the doubt that you want but take it from me, there's a fly in that ointment."

Ignoring that comment, Teyona said, "Can we just go now?"

Spending time with Russell; answering his questions, getting answers to hers and just getting to know him for Teyona that had made her life better. He'd made her begin to feel better about herself, that she shouldn't blame herself for things she had no control over. Knowing Russell had somehow allowed her to forgive herself which was something she hadn't been able to do before. But now, it appeared he was undoing all the good she'd seen in him and his brother and was beginning to wonder if he was playing some kind of sick game with her.

"You know if you really want to know what's going on in the examining room, it possible. I could show you."

"What? How?"

Russell pointed towards the building where Steven worked and the building beside it.

"You've been spying on Steven and his patients and you want me to participate in this nonsense? You can't be serious."

"I do and I am."

She looked at Russell as if he had three heads on his shoulders. "So you have been spying on my husband and his patients!"

Russell gave her a boyish grin, "I absolutely have been spying on your husband and his patients. I've been spying on everybody. That's why I'm here, remember?"

Exasperated, Teyona lifted her hands in the air and said, "Can we please just go?"

CHAPTER 23

STEVEN & RACHELLE

Steven agreed to keep his 'after hours' appointment with Rachelle. It had been weeks since they'd seen each other last and he hoped she'd changed her mind about bringing their son to Columbia to live.

He held the door open as Rachelle sauntered into his offices. Steven had to do a double-take. Rachelle was looking good, damn good he had to admit, and she smelled good too. But of course, any woman Steven dicked down had to be fine. He wasn't like some men who would fuck anything in a skirt and with a pulse. Hell, no. Steven Carter had standards.

Upon closing the door, Rachelle went for him. Furiously, her hands were all over him, but Steven took both her hands in his. It didn't stop Rachelle from attempting to free her hands in order to undress him so they could get down to business. He had to know whether she'd taken care of things on her end concerning their son. "Rachelle, stop," he commanded.

Rachelle's smile went dim, "Why?" she asked with a confused look on her face.

Steven steeled himself before he spoke, "Why? Because of our son. It's been a while since we discussed his situation and I want to know if you were able to find someone to keep him if your mother can't do it."

He released her hands and Rachelle's eyes lit up. She playfully traced his beard with her index finger before placing soft kisses down along his exposed chest as she made her way down to his manhood.

"Rachelle, stop!" he grabbed her hands tightly and stood her back up to face him. "I want to know if you have made arrangements for someone else besides your mother in North Carolina to take care of Stevie Jr."

"You ole meany," she pouted. "Denying me the good stuff."

Steven's eyes flashed angrily. He tightened his grip on her. "There's plenty of time for that."

"Okay, okay," she smiled, sexily. "Lucky for you, lover, I was able to find someone to take care of little Stevie."

"In North Carolina?" Steven quizzed, hoping that she would allow the boy to remain in North Carolina instead of bringing him to Columbia.

"Yes, in North Carolina," Rachelle rolled her eyes and replied petulantly, "But it's gonna cost you a pretty penny."

Steven released his grip on her and smiled brightly. "The money I'm not concerned about. My son deserves the best." He took Rachelle in his arms and gave her a big kiss, "And by the way, it's we who were lucky in this instance."

Rachelle snuggled up close to Steven. She whispered in his ear, "So does this mean that we can finally get down to my examination, Doctor? I need your expertise." She turned around in her outfit showing off her curves and other goodies before moving close to him again, grinding up against his body.

Steven watched her move appreciatively. Even though, he'd already been well sated by Abby merely hours before Rachelle arrived, he wasn't one to turn down one of his favorite past times with a beautiful woman. Rachelle dropped gracefully to her knees, unzipped his trouser and began stroking his manhood before placing it in her mouth. He reflected on his life. He'd just dodged a bullet with his son. That fact alone could have blown up in his face and tore his world apart. Then, there was his loving and trusting wife at home none the wiser to the bevy of beautiful women he had on the side to satisfy his sexual needs. What was more is that none of the side women knew about the others even though he'd been sleeping with some of them for years. Steven stared down at Rachelle as she began her work on his manhood and his face broke out in a huge grin. The thought occurred to him that he had got to be the luckiest man in the world.

CHAPTER 24

TEYONA & RUSSELL

Russell started up the car and they drove out of the parking lot. Teyona remained quiet along the way, but instead of driving her back to her car, Russell drove directly to his hotel. He pulled into a parking space and shut off the engine. She glanced around and looked over at him.

"Why are we here?" she asked, looking sternly over at him.

"I can tell that you've returned to having the worst opinion of me right now, but come on. I want to show you something," he said, getting out of the car, not waiting for her response.

Teyona didn't know what made her want to obey his request, but she did. She opened the door, got out of the car and entered the hotel with Russell. They rode the elevator up to his room in silence.

Russell opened the door to his room. Entering, he said, "Have a seat," motioning towards the couch. "Can I get you something to drink?"

"No," she replied, stiffly.

Russell went over to the mini bar to make himself a drink. "I'm gonna make you one anyway, just in case."

"Since you've gone to all this trouble to investigate the hell out of us, you may as well show me what you have uncovered," Teyona said, sitting on the couch, crossing her legs.

Russell had been observing her for months and while he knew she was a woman of incredible strength in spite of all she'd been through, he'd also seen a very sweet and vulnerable side of her so he didn't want to wound her more than she already had been which is why he hesitated so long to show her what he'd found out.

"Are you sure you are ready for what I've got to show you?" he said, carrying both drinks over and setting them on the coffee table before taking a seat on the couch next to Teyona.

"How can I know that until I see what you have?"

Russell had come to town to ruin everyone's lives connected directly or indirectly with the death of his brother. His intention was to make them pay, but after getting to know Teyona, he'd completely changed his mind. Still he had to make her aware of what was going on with her husband and her best friend so she could make the decision how she would handle it. Knowing Teyona, he knew she'd find the strength from within to do what she needed to do.

Russell had put all the pictures and videos together. All he had to do was press PLAY and all the images would be projected on the wall in his room. He looked intently at Teyona one last time before getting up from the couch and said, "You can change your mind if you want to."

She shook her head. "No, let me see what you have."

"Okay," Russell got up from the couch, walked over to hit the switch on the wall by the door, turning off the lights. The room was now semi-dark, with only a small amount of light filtering in from the bathroom. He returned to the couch and hit the PLAY button. In the next second, images of Steven and Abby, his young, sexy, blond nurse, were kissing in the patient examining room. Russell looked over at Teyona when the image of Abby, getting down on her knees, taking Steven's rock hard penis into her mouth and sucking hungrily on it while the look of pure ecstasy showed on Steven's face.

Teyona leaped from the couch. "Stop it! Stop it!" she screamed, walking over to the window to look out, only she didn't see anything outside. All she could see was the image of the look on her husband's face while Abby had his penis in her mouth. "Oh my God. How could he do this to me? How could they?" she said and begun to cry.

Russell shut off the device, quickly got up from the couch and went over to her with the drinks in hand. He handed one to her. She accepted it and took a healthy gulp from it. He removed a handkerchief from his pocket offering it to her upon taking it and using it to wipe away tears that kept repeating themselves rolling down her face, she wiped her nose.

"I know this is painful but you shouldn't be in the dark about what's going on right under your nose."

"You must think as a therapist that I am a complete fool to not have known that my husband was guilty of infidelity."

"No, I don't think that at all. I think that some of the people closest to you have been very deceitful, dishonest and uncaring. You can't be blame for caring about them. That's just who you are. Right now though, I think you need to see the rest of it. Take in all the pain now and when you have processed it all, you will be on the other side of it. And, believe me, you will be much better when this is all out in the open."

Teyona allowed Russell to lead her back over to the couch. They sat down together. He looked at her, she nodded her head in consent. He pressed the PLAY button on the device again and again, she was faced with staggering images of her husband being unfaithful to her. Unanswered questions bounced around in her mind. When did he start cheating on her? Why had he caused her to feel such guilt about what she'd done when he was doing the exact same thing?

"You okay?" Russell asked, leaning close to her.

How could she be with what was being presented to her? She nodded that she was okay.

Another image that appeared on the wall was Steven with Abby, having sex on the patient's bed in the examining room. Again, Teyona leaped from the couch with both hands up to her face and began pacing the floor. Russell set his drink glass on the table, placed his elbows on his upper thighs and rested his chin in his palms while watching Teyona. He saw her used the handkerchief again to wipe away tears from her face.

Russell couldn't deny his heart was breaking for this woman. A woman he barely knew yet he felt he knew her better than most. He wished he could take her in his arms and erase the pain that he knew was suffocating her heart, her entire body. Regaining her composure, Teyona returned to the couch and sat, determined that she wouldn't stop watching until she'd seen the last image, the last piece of footage.

Russell started running snapshot after snapshot. He could see her squirming in her seat but she didn't get up to dodge the images or looked away. Often times, she wiped tears from her face but she remained seated. He shut off the device and looked at her. "We can stop here if you want."

"No, I'm okay."

He nodded and other images appeared on the wall. He moved closer to her on the couch and he placed one arm around her shoulders. She didn't shake it off of her nor did she move away from him as they watched image after image of the sexual acts that appear on the wall.

It had already been established that Steven was a cheater but the next image, not only caught Teyona completely by surprised, it stunned her to her core.

Steven and Rachelle, hand in hand, entered the examining room and as soon as the door closed behind them, they were into each other's arms kissing passionately while tearing each other's clothes off. Teyona's hands flew to her mouth. Russell's arm tightened around her shoulders and they watched as Steven and Rachelle performed oral sex on each other with Teyona fighting a losing battle with tears that kept spilling out her eyes, streaming down her cheeks. She was almost hysterical now. Russell shut off the projector, wrapped both arms around her and held her tight in his arms, allowing her the time to do what she needed to do. He held her and rocked her back and forth as she sobbed uncontrollably. After a while, she stopped crying. He took the handkerchief from her hand and dabbed at her tears before putting the handkerchief on the table.

He did not start the device again until he was certain she was ready to go forward. It wasn't very long before she was ready to see the rest of what he had. The next image they saw was that of Steven laying Rachelle on the bed, his completely naked body mounting hers and shoving his manhood into her. Within seconds, they were having wild, unchecked, unbridled sex. Steven was giving to Rachelle, her best friend, what he'd promise to always keep for her and her alone. It was painful watching Steven having sex with his nurse but it was devastating watching him have sex with Rachelle who didn't appear to have any problem having sex with her best friend's husband.

"How long has this been going on?" she asked through her sobs.

"I don't know but you can see how completely comfortable they are with each other that this isn't something that just started," Russell said. He omitted telling Teyona that Rachelle had giddily admitted to him that she and Steven had been having an affair for years. He explained to her how he'd met Rachelle when he came to town and that it was she who agreed to work with him to bring her down, but he said, "My guess is that this has been going on a while."

Again, Teyona was at a loss for words. She just looked at him. After what seemed like an eternity, she said, between sobs, "I didn't realize that the person who I've considered my best friend for all these years hated me so much."

Russell held her eyes, his eyes full of sorrow, "She told me herself. She wants what you have. She wants your life."

"And she is willing to destroy me mentally to have it."

"Don't put all the blame on her. I played a huge part in the plan. As a matter of fact, it was I who put the plan into action. So we can't put all the blame on her."

"Now, who's defending who? I can't believe you're defending her. No matter what kind of plan you approached her with she should not have had any part in it. Had someone approached me with something against her, they could've gone straight to hell. I would never have been a part of anything that would cause harm to her."

"That's what a real friend would do." He concluded.

Teyona was seething when she said, "I could kill her." And, she meant that too.

The next set of pictures that was displayed on the wall was Steven and Rachelle, minutes apart, entering the same hotel and later leaving that same way. He didn't need pictures, slides or videos for Teyona to know what went on in the hotel room they occupied. It was all there before her eyes, yet she couldn't believe it, didn't want to believe it. Then, an image of Steven and Rachelle together appeared on the wall. No one had to use their imagination or guess what was going on in that image. It was perfectly clear. They were having raw, fierce, animalistic sex and Teyona could clearly see how each was enjoying it.

Russell drew his attention from the images on the wall back to Teyona and she had both hands up to her face. She hadn't only been shocked by what she'd seem, she'd been devastated. For some time, she'd been trying to convince herself that Steven had forgiven her and was moving forward with their relationship, their marriage. Only he hadn't. He'd been carrying on affairs with Rachelle, Abby. . . and other women. She'd no idea how many other women.

For the next twenty minutes or so, they watched pictures and videos of Steven and whoever he happened to be with when Russell was investigating

him, and they talked in between. After the last slide
was shown, Teyona got up from the couch and
walked back over to the window.

"I have one last thing to tell you."

"I don't know if I can handle anything else."

Russell knew he had to tell her something that
would hurt her more than anything she'd seen or
heard today. "Do you remember a while back when
Rachelle left town to go visit her mother?"

"Yes, she wasn't happy with some things at
work. She said she'd played it right though because
she took a year off from work and when she
returned, she received a huge promotion." Teyona
said, dismissively.

"Well," Russell began not looking at her. "She
went back home to have a child."

Her head snapped up.

"Your husband's child. The child is now over a
year old."

For a moment, Teyona looked as if she was
going to faint but immediately she composed
herself, turned to him and asked, "What did you just
say?"

"Dr. Carter and your friend are the parents of a
son, Steven Jr."

"Are you serious? Rachelle has a son, with
Steven. Are you sure? I mean are you sure that
Steven is the father." Deep inside her she knew
what Russell was telling her was true and before he
answered, she whispered, "Steven and Rachelle
have a child together! Oh my goodness. I don't
believe it. I can't believe any of this. I just can't."

"I know how you feel but everything I've shown you is true. I am certain of that." Russell rummaged through some folders and presented Teyona with a North Carolina Certificate of Live Birth.

Teyona dragged herself to the nearest chair where she nearly collapsed into it. The birth certificate identified Rachelle as the mother and Steven as the father of a healthy six pound, three ounce baby boy.

"This is just too much," she mumbled, although she held the proof in her hands, then she added, her voice shaking, "Why is this happening? Why?" She looked at Russell, her eyes pleading. "I can't go home tonight. Would you mind if I stayed here with you? I'll sleep on the couch."

"Yes, you can stay here and no, you will not sleep on the couch. You can sleep over there." He pointed towards the Queen sized bed. I'll sleep on the couch."

Teyona had an urge to protest. She didn't want the man to give up his bed for her but she was too exhausted, too emotionally spent to argue. She raised her hands and said, "Alright," before her hands limply fell back to her side. Walking slowly back over to the coffee table, she lifted her glass to her mouth and finished her drink before she dragged herself over to the bed and fell on it. Call Rachelle, she thought. Anytime something of this magnitude happened in her life, she'd call Rachelle and she always felt better talking things through with her. This time, there would be no calling Rachelle. How could she? There was no way Rachelle could help her with a solution when she was a major part of the problem.

Sometime during the night, Russell heard sobs and he recalled that he wasn't in the room alone. Teyona was there with him. He'd had several additional shots last night before lying on the couch and drifting off into a troubled sleep and he was still feeling the residual effects of the alcohol hours later. He'd seen many images that night but the one he couldn't get out of his head was the one of Teyona, her entire body wracked with pain. And though he'd not caused the pain directly, his indirect actions contributed greatly to that pain.

Russell looked towards the bed. In the semi-dark room, he could see that she was crying. "Are you alright?" he asked and immediately wanted to kick himself for asking such a lame question. If she was alright, she wouldn't be crying. He got up from the couch, went to the sink and filled a glass with water that he took over to the bed where she was. She sat up on the side of the bed, took the glass from his hand, and after taking several swallows, she said, "I didn't mean to wake you. I'm sorry."

"Don't worry about that," he said, sitting on the bed next to her and instinctively reaching up to smooth her hair away from her face.

Teyona took another sip from the glass and placing the glass on the night table, she shook her head. She had a reputation for fixing other people's problems no matter how complex but here she was uncertain that she could help herself. Posing the question to Russell, she asked, "What am I going to do?"

He placed his arm around her shoulders and pulled her close so she could lean on him, draw strength from him if that was what she needed, and cried as long as she wanted, needed to. After a short while, she leaned away to look into his eyes.

"I'm so sorry that I killed your brother. I'm sorry I took him away from you, I'm sorry. I'm deeply sorry. If I could give your brother back to you, I would, I promise you I would," she said and sobbed some more.

"I know. I know," Russell said and Teyona noticed tears gathering in his eyes that began running down his face. Her heart went out to him and in that instance, she forgot her own problems. She'd been too caught up in what was going on in her life to even think about what Russell might be experiencing. The man had lost his brother, for goodness sakes, his twin brother. There weren't many losses greater than that. Losing a twin must be like losing a piece of yourself.

Teyona turned in Russell's arm so she could face him and wrapped both arms around him. His arms involuntary encircled her body in return. They held each other, crying together, experiencing unimaginable pain, brought on by different reasons but pain nonetheless and through that pain, their bond began to grow stronger. Once the tears were over, they released each other and looking deeply into each other's eyes, their eyes locked. And as their gaze continued, desire for Russell flooded her, wanting him to assault every inch of her body with his hands, his mouth and his manhood making her forget the pain, even for a short while. He must have read her unspoken desire in her eyes for in the next instance, Russell pulled Teyona into his arms and before even he realized what he was doing or she could stop him, his mouth covered hers in an earth shattering kiss. He thrust his tongue inside her mouth and within seconds, their tongues dueled until they were both gasping for breath. Teyona was the most captivating woman he'd ever met, and he'd known numerous women, and kissing her was electrifying.

Kissing on the bed together, Russell's body responded to their kisses, moving on her in a sexy fashion. Teyona's hands traveled across his broad back, down to his waist and his thighs, wanting to feel the heat and rhythm against her body. Teyona broke the kiss and stood up from the bed, pulling him along with her. She knew what she was feeling and it went against everything she believed in except she didn't care. She no longer had a reason to. She'd ended the affair with Bobby Johnson, vowing she'd never betray her husband or do anything that would betray or embarrassed him or her and their family again and she'd meant it. Only when she made those promises she hadn't expected to encounter what she had in the past several hours. Moreover, she'd never expected to meet the duplicate of the one and only man who'd touched her in such a way that would cause her to cheat on her husband in the first place. Despite her misgivings, she was overcome suddenly with the need to touch Russell and when she looked at him, amazingly she saw him and only him—not his brother. Then, seemingly without her permission, her arms raised up to his broad shoulders. She allowed her fingers to tighten on the hard muscle as his arms glided around her trim waist. He couldn't stop himself from pulling her roughly to him.

His face buried in her hair, he whispered, "I told you before that I see how Bobby was able to fall so deeply in love with you and I believe I am there myself. As a matter of fact, I know that I am. Please forgive me but I am in love with you. I know you are married and you are in love with that jackass who calls himself *your husband* but that's how I feel."

Teyona didn't respond. She didn't want to talk. She didn't want to be reminded that she was married to Steven and she definitely didn't want to think about Russell's twin brother. Perhaps when the sun came up, in the light of day, she might be able to think clearer but for now, she was in the arms of a man who was now trying to do nothing more than help her through painful betrayals and it was exactly where she wanted to be. She opened her legs to allow him to position himself between them and grind hard against her very intimate, her very personal, feminine spot.

Russell had been with numerous women and he had lots of sexual experiences but he'd never felt for anyone what he was feeling for Teyona. Incredibly, these feelings had not just begun. He began having strong feelings for her shortly after they met and despite her marital status, her position in her community and the country, instead of those feelings diminishing, they were growing.

As they kissed, Russell's head spun. They began ripping off each other's clothes and almost instantaneously, they were completely naked, kissing passionately, caressing furiously and gyrating powerfully against each other. His mouth left hers and slid down to the swell of her breasts. He let his tongue circle around one swollen nipple, then the other. He flicked his tongue, teasing and licking; one nipple then the other. He bit gently on a nipple, then placed a kiss on it before he soothed the spot with his tongue. His warm breath caressed the harden pebble and he heard a sharp intake of breath seconds before his mouth clamped down hard on her breast. He began to lick, bite and suck on her nipples, gently at first, then in the next moment he was feasting upon her breasts. His mouth, progressing at a frantic pace, alternating from one to the other; licking, biting, sucking hungrily, giving each breast equal treatment, until she thought she would go completely insane.

His opened mouth returned to hers, wildly excited, she thrust her tongue deep inside his mouth with thorough, hot sweeps. Teyona's passion was building rapidly. It was building with a force that left her gasping in anticipation as they stepped closer to the line that she'd vowed she'd never cross again. As he lowered himself to her, she ran her hand along his hard back and down until she reached his buttocks. She held him there. As the kiss intensified, she opened her legs wider and wider. He kissed her again before his mouth left hers and traveling down her body to her center where his tongue dipped into her, tasting her love. He mouthed her and went after her ardently, passionately, fiercely, enjoying all she gave him and all she allowed him to take.

Progressing back up her smooth, shapely body, she felt his harden penis penetrate her feminine core and she lifted her hips from the bed, rising up to meet him, urging him, welcoming him to take all he wanted from her and as his muscular, pulsating body joined with hers, he raised himself over her on his elbows and began to thrust in and out of her, all the while going harder , faster and deeper. He kissed her forehead, the tip of her nose, and the tears from her face before his mouth returned to hers. She wanted him to have her, take all that she had, all that he wanted. As they mated with each other, passionately, furiously, relentlessly, she discovered that she'd wanted him more than she'd thought was possible to want anyone.

Russell had never wanted anyone in his entire life the way he wanted Teyona and he wasn't just going to prove to her how much he wanted her, needed her, loved her—he would leave no doubt. His mouth found her earlobe that he gently sucked on. His tongue snaked its way into her ear and he heard her gasp as he licked her there. His tongue slipped into her mouth again finding hers, he sucked furiously on it. While Russell plunged relentlessly .

239

into her, she thrashed her hips recklessly up to meet his rhythm. He switched positions with Teyona, allowing her to be on top. She rode him as hard as she could; thrilling and exciting him, bringing all of his senses to a throbbing and glorious rapture that he'd never experienced before. She took from him what she wanted and gave to him what he needed. After a while, he rolled back on top and grinded against her in a way that was intoxicating. That night he declared his love for her easily, so unexpectedly. As he continued plunging into her, she bounced under him, her legs wrapped tightly around him, clutching him with all her strength. Her eyes closed in mindless ecstasy. She didn't relax her grip on him until each had reached the ultimate peak and their bodies went limp.

In the morning, Teyona woke in Russell's bed and his arms. He was already awake. "Good morning," he said, when he noticed her stirring in his embrace.

"How are you?" she responded.

"I am good," he replied snuggling even closer to her. "I hope you don't feel that I took advantage of you last night. All I can say is that I have no excuse for what happened. I'm crazy about you and I wanted you. I know I should have exercised more will power but I didn't have the strength." He stroked her cheek, "You're definitely my greatest weakness."

"Don't beat yourself up too much," she began softly. "What happened last night wasn't all your fault. If anyone's to blame, we have to start with ourselves. I was there too, remember." She said, stroking his broad chest.

Russell pulled her deeper into his chest. As they lay together, Teyona knew that after making love with Russell, once just wasn't enough. They were going to have sex again because she had to have Russell again. Once could never be enough for her with a man like Russell. It wasn't long before she felt her need for him rising and he was between her legs again, plunging fiercely into her while her head thrash about on the pillow. Somewhere deep inside she knew she was betraying her husband, had betrayed her husband last night when she made love to Russell, yet she felt no guilt and she felt even less as they were making love now.

Later, Teyona asked, "What will you do now?"

"Well, I've done what I came here to do with respect to my brother and I can now put that to rest, but I've got one more little thing I need to tie up."

"Anything to do with me," she wanted to know.

"No."

"That's good because I have had enough to last a lifetime. I suppose you will leave when that is done."

"I don't know," he replied, hoping she would ask him to stay in a town a while. He wanted Teyona to ask him to stay but knowing what was ahead of her, he knew she couldn't. So instead, he offered, "I don't know what you're gonna do about Dr. Carter and Rachelle but I'd love to be here and support you through whatever it is."

Teyona frowned, "I don't have any answers to all the questions that are floating around inside my head right now. When someone shows you who they are, whether you want to or not, you have to believe them and once that person deceives you with his character, there isn't much left." She looked thoughtful a moment. "But like I said, I don't know. I have a lot to think about."

CHAPTER 25

TEYONA & STEVEN

That Saturday morning, Russell had driven Teyona back to the underground garage to collect her vehicle. Arriving home, she parked her car and shut off the ignition. For a while, she didn't get out of her car. She just stared at her house and the tears flowed freely. This was the beginning of the end for her marriage and her friendship with Rachelle. She felt like a fool. All of this going on right under her nose. She could slap herself silly. Looking back, it was so obvious. How could she have missed it, how could she have been so blind? And to think she thought all this time she was working to earn Steven's trust back because she had betrayed him. How could he be so cruel? Teyona stopped blaming herself and finally got out of her car, walking the few steps to her house. She couldn't avoid the confrontation with Steven forever. She gathered her resolved and entered her house through the kitchen door.

Upon hearing the opening door, Steven leapt to his feet from where he was sitting at the kitchen table. He rushed over to his wife.

"There you are," he said nervously and asked, "Are you alright? Come, sit." He led her to a chair but she didn't sit. "You want some coffee? I just made a pot," he tried to cut through the tension he felt surrounding them.

Teyona looked at Steven coldly. "No, I don't want coffee, Steven" Teyona sneered.

"Where have you been, Teyona? When you didn't come home last night, I was worried sick about you."

Teyona's eyebrow arched up, "Did you call the police, the hospitals?"

"Well, no, I didn't," Steven said as if at a loss for words.

"Why not?" Teyona asked, with hands on her hip. "I mean, I'm your wife and I didn't come home last night. I've never done anything like that before and you didn't try to find out if something had happened to me?"

Steven was really at a loss for words now. He knew his wife knew something but not sure what. He wouldn't show his hand, he'd let her tell him.

"Come and talk to me. Tell me what's bothering you." He was about to put his arms around her until he saw the look of agony on her face. What's wrong?" He asked subconsciously knowing the answer. The concern on Steven's face was more for him than it was for Teyona. Had she found out some of his secrets that he would've given his right

244

arm to have kept hidden? His mind began to race. What does she know? He wondered. How much does she know and more importantly, who told her whatever it was that'd gotten her so upset. He really didn't have to think long or hard for the answers to his questions because he thought he knew exactly who it had been! Rachelle! "That fucking bitch!" he muttered. Then he asked again, "Baby, please, talk to me."

Teyona closed her eyes briefly. She held up a hand as if it was a stop sign. "Steven, don't even try it," she hissed through clenched teeth, her eyes now boring into his. "I know everything so don't you try to lie and talk your way out of what you've done."

"Okay," he began, knowing this could turn into a volatile situation. His mind raced with what he could do to diffuse it fast. Maybe she didn't know what he thought. it could be something trivial but not to her. He could only hope. His marriage was at stake. "Tell me what it is that you think you know," Steven said, grasping at straws. He knew his wife wasn't a liar or much for the dramatics either; therefore, whatever she knew and was about to accuse him of was a sure bet it had happened. "Let's talk."

"Don't. Don't." Teyona raised her hand in the air and looked at Steven with disbelief. "Seriously, Steven, what are we gonna talk about? Who are you? I don't even know who the fuck I married or how I could have been so blind all these years to not see what you were doing to me." Her voice began to rise, "So you tell me. What are we going to talk

245

about? You fucking your nurse, Abby, in your office," she quipped heatedly, her lips curled down and disgust written all over her face. "And," she continued, "who knows how many others."

She went on telling Steven more of what she knew until he interrupted her.

"What about you?" Steven had to stop her. He felt he was drowning. "You weren't completely innocent in all of this. Granted, I may have fucked more people than you, but that doesn't make me more guilty by no means. You are just as guilty as I am."

"You are right. I am guilty. But what you did to me was unfathomable." She paused glaring at him. "You know what hurt me the most?" She got up close and personal in Steven's face. "The thing that hurt me most is the fact that you are fucking Rachelle, the woman who for years I thought was my friend, my best friend. Oh, yes, I am guilty of sleeping with someone else. Um hum," her head bobbed up and down in agreement, "but I didn't fuck your best friend," she said poking a finger at his chest. "Never in a million years would I have fucked one of your friends." Teyona paused to take in a long breath before she continued. "This woman was more like a sister to me than a friend and the two of you have been carrying on this torrid affair w-a-a-y before I even knew Bobby Johnson existed." She drew out the word 'way' before throwing up both hands to the sky and shaking her head, "and I absolutely had no clue." She pointed a finger accusingly at him wagging it in his face.

246

"What you did and have been doing all along had nothing to do with your distress over my being unfaithful. You have been acting on your own character for years. This is just who you are, a natural born liar and cheater. Even if I hadn't known any of the Bobby Johnsons of the world, you would have still been this nasty ass, can't keep your dick in his pants, cheating ass, son of a bitch that you are." Steven wanted to say something but changed his mind when Teyona gave him the evil eye.

In all the years they'd been together, Steven had never heard Teyona use such harsh language. "I am supposed to know people, get inside their minds, see their thoughts, get a handle on their issues and help to solve them. I had a storm brewing all around me and I had no idea that I was in its eye." She laughed bitterly. "I guess you two must have had a great time, laughing at me behind my back, calling me the proverbial fool that I am." She paused, head down gripping a chair, gathering the strength to utter the next words, "But worst of all," she raised her head, eyes gleaming with fury, voice low, "you and Rachelle have a child together." Steven flinched. "You gave Rachelle a child, a son." Teyona paused again to take another deep breath. She shook her head again, thinking of the irony of the situation, "Rachelle wouldn't even fulfill her own husband's wishes and give him a child and we both know how much George wanted a child. But, because of her jealousy, her hatred of me and wanting my life, she purposefully allowed *you* to get her pregnant and have *your* child." Speaking as if she was talking more to herself than to Steven, she added, "I don't understand what is it about my life she is so jealous of? She's a gorgeous woman with a man who loves her so, so much that he would do anything for her. She has a great job, a beautiful home and they are not hurting at all financially. What more could she possibly want? She's a fool thinking she can do better than George but that's just my opinion because obviously she felt you were better." She cut her eyes towards Steven, pausing before she said, "I can't believe the two of you would hurt me this way." She choked back a sob that threatened to erupt at any moment. She placed her hand on the counter top of the island to steady herself as she took another deep, measuring breath, not only to calm her nerves but to quiet her quickly mounting fury again.

"I feel badly for George because he loves Rachelle so much. All he's ever wanted to do was love her, take care of her, be successful and make her proud of him, but the silly *bitch* couldn't even appreciate that. But, I know George. This is gonna be a setback for him but he's strong. He's gonna be alright and if he needs someone to talk to, to help him through this, I'll be there for him because George is my friend and I don't want him to become stuck, not trust people and miss out of true happiness. I'll let him know that love and happiness will come again and when it does, that he should take a chance and grab it because we never know what life will throw at us."

Teyona heard a noise escape Steven's opened mouth. He was thinking of the kind of person she was. Here she was, her life was shattered around her feet but she was thinking of ways to help someone else. So unselfish, such an amazing human being, he thought. Why did he have to screw that up! Why!

She continued, "This last year, I have lived each day with the guilt of betraying you, Steven, all I wanted to do was make it up to you. Get back to us being the family that I thought we were but I was wrong. I am in no way trying to minimize what I did because what I did was wrong but what you did was wrong as well. You found little subtle ways to make me feel guilty. That was what you wanted to do to me, and I accepted it because I felt I deserved it, but I know now that I didn't. Yes, I was guilty of betraying you but I didn't deserve the guilt you lavished on me almost daily. All while your ass was out screwing damn near every woman that crossed your path. How cruel can you be? You sadistic bastard! You knew I was in pain and your goal was to keep me in that bottomless pit of pain, agony and guilt." She brushed away the tears that slipped from her eyes as she continued to hurl all of what she knew at him. After Teyona finally finished telling him everything she knew, she added, "If Rachelle wants my life with you, she can have it because I'm done! You two deserve each other. So you see, there's nothing left for us to talk about. I just want you to get your things and I want you out of this house. I want you gone," she said, pointing a finger towards the door. "And Rachelle! I'll deal with that trick later. Believe that." With a look of revulsion all over her face, Teyona turned and walked away from him. At the door, she turned and looked at him, with tears streaming down her cheeks. The look she gave him cut to his core, his very essence. If looks could kill! However, her next words caught Steven by surprise when she asked, "How could you, Steven? How could you do this to me? How."

All these years Teyona thought Steven had loved her, only her and in spite of what she'd done, she never once thought he would hurt me, but he had. The one thing she knew he would never do he had done with Rachelle, her best friend. She could never have betrayed Steven or Rachelle in that way with someone she knew or loved. Never!

Teyona left Steven in the kitchen and climbed the stairs in slow motion, going up to take a long, hot shower. She wished the hot spray of the shower could wash away the disappointment, the pain and the dirt she felt had attached itself to her, knowing what she now knew. He watched her until she disappeared upstairs. He knew he'd been caught, had been found out. Everything Teyona said to him was true, but he loved his wife. He loved her more than any other living thing in his entire life and he didn't want to lose her. He wanted Teyona, he wanted their marriage. But with all that had happened, with all that she'd learned about him, could he save their marriage? Would she ever forgive him? Would their lives ever be the same? Steven inhaled deeply, then blew out a huge puff of air and brushed a tear that slipped from his eye. Maybe in time, when some of the hurt was gone, there might still be a chance for them because they loved each other like no other, he thought. In the next moment, his anger flared. Why would Rachelle go to Teyona with this? Hadn't he warned her to keep all this away from Teyona? Wasn't the situation with their son settled?

"I should have never trusted that bitch. I knew she was gonna fuck everything up! Everything!" he said dropping down hard in his chair with his head in his hands.

Sometime later, Steven picked himself up from his chair and went upstairs. At the top of the stairs, he heard the sound of the shower coming from one of the spare bedrooms. He paused momentarily at that closed door before he turned and went into their bedroom. He removed a large suitcase from the closet and began packing some clothes. Within the hour, Steven went back downstairs with his suitcase in one hand, his briefcase in the other and another small bag hung from his shoulder.

As he reached for the door knob, he turned at the sound of Teyona's voice behind him. She'd showered and changed into slacks, a cream sleeveless blouse, flat shoes and no makeup. She said, "I need you to give me a day's notice when you plan to come back to get the rest of your things because I don't want to be here when you do. I never want to see your face again." Soon after, she added, "And, no, Steven, I'm not the fool you and Rachelle think that I am. I just happened to have cared so much for my husband and best friend that it just didn't occur to me that you'd ever deceive me."

Steven was in more emotional pain than he'd ever experience in his entire life and he didn't know how to handle it. If he didn't love his wife so much, it wouldn't have hurt so badly. He nodded, looked down at his feet and he left the house through the kitchen door.

CHAPTER 26

STEVEN & RACHELLE

He went over to his car, opened the trunk and threw his bags and briefcase into it. He got into the car, backed out from the garage and with squealing wheels, left the house. He pulled his phone from his pant pocket and hit the button to place a call. When the call connected, he shouted furiously, "What the fuck do you think you're doing? Do you have any idea what you have done to my family, my marriage, my life?" He didn't wait for her to answer before he added, "Fucking bitch, you've ruined me."

On the other end of the phone, Rachelle wondered how Steven knew she'd brought their son to town. Nothing else would've made him so angry and he was angry. Well, she thought, she didn't care that he knew or that he was angry. He wasn't going to tell her what to do or how she should handle the situation involving their son. "What are you talking about, Steven?" she asked, feigning ignorance.

Steven wasn't going to play these games with her. She'd already done too damn much damage and he was furious with her. "I'll be at the hotel in fifteen minutes. Get your ass over there." Steven ended the call and threw the phone, sending it sailing against the dashboard. For years, Rachelle had been making moves on him, literally throwing herself at him, but he'd denied her until three years ago. He'd tried to keep her at bay but she was so determined that she broke through his resistance and he'd caved in to her advances. It'd started the night he and Teyona were hosting a surprise birthday party at their home for George. Teyona wanted a special bottle of George's favorite champagne for their toast later that evening. She and Rachelle were putting the finishing touches on the decorations when Steven came in from work.

Noticing Steven was empty handed, Teyona asked, "Honey, is the champagne in the car?"

Forgetting to pick up the bottle of champagne on the way home, he face-palmed and stated, "Oh gosh, I forgot." Turning to go back out the door, he said, "I'll go right now and pick up a bottle."

Teyona rushed up to him giving him a quick peck on his lips and said, "No, babe, you're just getting home from work. Take a few minutes and catch your breath. I'll run out and pick up a bottle."

"Are you sure?" he asked, a wrinkle in his brow. "Because I don't mind."

"Yeah, I'll be right back," she replied and turning to Rachelle, said, "We'll have time to change when I get back. Don't forget the meatballs in the oven."

"I won't," Rachelle said, busy tying streamers on balloons.

Teyona grabbed her purse and keys and rushed out the door.

"So how was your day?" Rachelle asked Steven.

"Busy but not so bad," he answered, going over to the cabinet to make himself a drink.

As he leaned over to get a bottle of Scotch from the rack, he felt a body pressing against his. He quickly turned but before he could stop her, Rachelle had wrapped her arms around his neck, pinning him against the counter and stabbing her tongue inside his mouth. She immediately began grinding hard against him. She swirled her tongue around in his mouth, then stabbed it deeper and deeper inside.

After allowing his tongue to briefly mate with hers, Steven broke away and said, "Rachelle, what are you doing? You know we can't do this."

"Why not?" She asked innocently. "We are adults. I want you and," her hand snaked down to his manhood that was betraying him by the seconds, growing longer, harder and more powerful, "I can tell you want me too. Your friend is telling me so right now." She grinned up in his face as she began to unzip his pants. His attempt to stop her was weak at best. Ignoring his feeble attempts, Rachelle reached into Steven's pants and pulled out his massive, hard penis. Her eyes danced at the enormity of it. She began to slide her hand up and down on his shaft, feeling it grow humongous.

Wow! What a man! She thought. She pulled up the long flare dress she was wearing, lifted her foot onto the handle of the cabinet drawer and tipping on one foot, placed the head of his rock, hard penis at the entry of her center and began to move against him. In the next instant, he lifted her from the floor. Both her legs went up around his waist as he pushed himself into her as fierce as he could. After a while, they dropped to the floor, and he began to plunge into her savagely, brutally, unmercifully.

"Oh, Steven," she moan. "That's right, baby, give it to me. You don't know how long I've waited for this. Please, please, pleaseeeeee," she said in a continuous plea.

Steven continued to plow down hard into her all the while hoping his wife wouldn't walk through the door.

Later when Teyona returned, Rachelle was downstairs doing whatever she was doing with the balloons while Steven was upstairs taking a shower. Since that time, they'd continued to meet several times a month, mostly at Rachelle's insistence. He knew now that he never should've gotten involved with that woman. He'd known Rachelle well enough to know that she was bad news; she was an emotional creature, the type of woman who acted on her emotions and people who acted on their emotions were dangerous! Translation! Rachelle was dangerous! Well, if she thought she was dangerous, he would introduce her to some real danger and the sooner the better.

Steven sped through the busy Saturday morning traffic, arriving at the hotel where he and Rachelle had met on numerous occasions. He drove around the hotel parking lot until he saw her car. He parked on the opposite side of the parking lot, gathered his things from the car trunk and entered the hotel where Rachelle would have already called and booked a room as she usually did when they met to avoid having him use his name. Upon entering the hotel, Steven saw Rachelle getting into one of the elevators. At the same time, his phone rang. It was her giving him the room number. He rode up to the desired floor finding the door ajar when he approached it. Suddenly the door flew open, Steven walked into the room and after closing the door and dropping his bags and briefcase to the floor, he caught Rachelle by her arm, flung her down on the bed and he landed on top of her with his hands around her throat. "Didn't I tell you to stay away from my wife with this shit? Didn't I tell you that?"

Rachelle twisted and turned, trying to pry Steven's hands away from her throat. Gasping, she squeaked out in a whispered, "I don't know what you're talking about." When he didn't release his grip on her, she removed one hands from his and began fighting him; she scratched and kicked and clawed, finally punching him hard in the nose. Blood shot over her face, her clothes, and the bed.

Pain ripped through his face, then shot up to the top of his head. He sprung off of her, his nose in his

257

hands. He lowered his hands to see blood spilling from between his fingers, he said, "Did you just break my fucking nose?" rushing off to the bathroom. He returned later to the bedroom, with a wad of tissue up to his nose. Rachelle was sitting on the side of the bed, rubbing her throat with one hand while using the other to wipe his blood from her face with tissues from the box on the nightstand. "Why are you behaving like this, Steven?" she yelled at him.

"How many times have I told you that we had to be careful?" Steven said, obviously still angry but in a calmer voice. "Now she knows everything and kicked me out of the house. What the fuck were you thinking?" He glared at her.

"I still don't know what you are talking about. I haven't told Teyona a damn thing," Rachelle snapped angrily at the tone he'd used with her earlier and the way he was treating her now, though she was smiling internally. A thought entered her mind and began to take hold, she said slowly, "That's why she phoned me a little while ago, calling me all kinds of names, telling me that I'm the worst kind of bitch and that she'd see that I get mine. I tried talking to her to ask her what she was talking about, but she hung up and when I tried to call her back, my calls went straight to voice mail."

"Don't you lie to me," Steven said, in a menacing tone, removing the wad of tissues from his nose to look at before tossing them into the trash.

"I'm not lying to you, Steven. I don't know what she knows. I just know I haven't told her anything."

"Are you trying to tell me you didn't tell my wife about you and me, and the baby?" he asked, sarcastically, a scowl on his angry, handsome face.

"I haven't told your wife a thing." Rachelle said, irritated. She hadn't said a word to Teyona although for years, she'd wanted to, and as far as she knew, she was one of only two people who were privy to that information; she and Steven. There was also Russell. He was an investigator after all. He could have tip Teyona off. He knew about her affair with Steven, hell, she had told him. But she didn't tell him anything about their son. That man was good, though. The information he uncovered as a result of his investigations were spot on. He'd learned far more than she'd told him.

As Steven stalked around the room, firing one hateful look after another in her direction, he angrily told her everything that Teyona had told him. He couldn't tell Rachelle where Teyona had gotten her information but he didn't have to. Rachelle already knew. She knew exactly who told Teyona all that she knew. It'd been Russell and as she looked at Steven, she knew it was time to lower the boom on his ass. She said, "I know who told Teyona about us."

Steven stared at her incredulously. "What are you talking about? How do you know who told Teyona? How would you know that? What's going on here?" he asked, walking over to the bed where she was.

"It was Russell," Rachelle said, throwing bloody tissues into the trash.

"Russell? Who the hell is Russell?" He wanted to know.

"Russell Andrew Johnson."

Part of the name rang a bell with Steven. He told Rachelle that he remembered coming home from work early one afternoon when a man was leaving his house. Questioning Teyona, she indicated the man was a client whose name was Russell Andrew. "That was all she'd said."

"Well, his name is Russell Andrew Johnson. He is Bobby Johnson's twin brother," she said and watched Steven's face transform with the knowledge of who the man was who had secretly visited his wife, in their home.

Steven glared at Rachelle and said, "That was Teyona former lover's twin brother?"

Rachelle nodded in consent.

"What the hell was Bobby Johnson's twin brother doing in my house?"

"Russell Andrew Johnson came to town to find out what happened to his brother."

Steven walked over to a chair, pulled it up close to the bed and sat down. "I want you to tell me everything that you know about this man; where does he come from," he enumerated on his fingers. "When did he come to town, how long has he been here, what he does for a living? Is he some kind of cop? I want to know everything that you know about him and Rachelle, don't leave anything out?"

Rachelle told Steven everything she knew about Bobby Johnson's brother. When she finished, she looked at Steven. "He just happened to tell Teyona before I did," she said under her breath.

"What did you just say?" Steven glared at Rachelle.

"I didn't say anything," she lied, but it was her sly smile that upset him.

He got up from the chair and gave her a long, ominous look before he said, "I want you to leave. I need some time alone."

"Don't you want to see your son, our son?" she asked waiting for the fall out.

Steven's eyes pierced into hers. "What do you mean? Where is he? Did you bring him here?" the questions rolled out of his mouth.

Rachelle nodded.

"You told me that you'd found someone in North Carolina to take care of the boy," he said, heatedly.

She shrugged her shoulders nonchalantly, "I lied."

Steven glared at her seconds before slapping her across the face, sending her backwards on the bed. "You just did what the fuck you wanted to do, huh? Where is he?" Steven yelled. She was wailing but he didn't care. "Where is he?" he repeated, only louder.

"He's at a friend's house," she managed to get out between sniffles.

"When did you bring the boy here?"

"This morning," she replied and again, Steven noticed the sly grin on her face although tears streamed down her face.

Steven didn't say anything further. He shook his head and continued to glare at her. "Fucking loose cannon," he hissed.

CHAPTER 27

TEYONA

Broken hearted as she ascended the stairs, Teyona was very sad, lonely and scared, and for the first time in her adult life, Teyona was uncertain what she was going to do with the rest of her life. She had no plan, no direction. How would she navigate through the overwhelming pain that she was experiencing?

With a box of tissues in her hand, Teyona entered the den, walked slowly over to the French doors leading to the terrace and stared out at the rain pouring outside. She brushed tears from her eyes as she watched raindrops splashed causing ripples in their backyard pool. The box of tissues fell from her hand to the floor as she lifted both hands up to her face and began to cry.

Still sobbing, Teyona pulled herself up from the floor, opened the French doors and walked out on the terrace. The rain was coming down hard. She stood, with her face tilted towards the sky mingling her tears with the rain that lashed at her face. "Why would they do this to me? How could they hurt me like this? How could you, Steven? How could you?" she screamed as she sobbed, falling on her knees to the floor where she wept uncontrollable.

Almost a half hour later, she returned inside the house, her clothes saturated, thoroughly drenches. She walked across the hall to the stairs, leaving a trail of water from her wet clothes, behind her. Earlier, she'd moved some of her things from the bedroom she'd shared with her husband. She would now occupy another bedroom. It would be sometime before she'd sleep in that room again, if ever. She went into the adjoining bathroom to her current bedroom, ran water in the tub and poured in some scented bubble bath before she climbed into the hot sudsy water and reclining in the tub, her head resting against the bath pillow. The house appeared unusually quiet. Though Steven was away from home often and she was at home alone, for some reason the quiet was unnerving.

She turned and pressed the button to the stereo system that she kept tuned in to an easy listening station. She caught the end of Toni Braxton's 'Unbreak My Heart.' Teyona ran a sudsy hand along her forehead, wishing she'd brought a glass of wine upstairs with her. The next song playing filled the bathroom with the soulful sounds of Dionne Warwick's 'I Know I'll Never Love This Way Again.'

Teyona's cell phone rang, breaking the spell she was immersed in. She looked around for it, then remembered it was in the pants pocket she was wearing and gotten completely wet. It appears the rain hadn't damage her phone. However it didn't matter. She wasn't interested in talking to anyone, especially not Steven or Rachelle.

Almost an hour later, Teyona stepped out of the bathtub, toweled herself dry and slipped into a white, silk robe. She removed her phone from the wet jeans that she picked up from the floor, stuck her feet into her bedroom slippers and carried the wet items downstairs to the laundry room.

It was late Saturday afternoon when Teyona entered the kitchen hungry, realizing she hadn't eaten anything all day. She laid her phone on the counter, pulled a frying pan from the cabinet, set it on the stove and removed eggs and butter from the refrigerator. She dropped two slices of bread into the toaster and cracked open a couple of eggs along with a pat of butter into the frying pan. She sat at the table, spread jam on the toast and poured a cup of herbal tea. After eating two forks of eggs and one bite of toast, she pushed her plate away, got up from the table and after scraping the uneaten foot into the garbage disposal and setting her plate in the sink, she picked up her phone and teacup and carried them with her into the den. She sat on the couch and placed her phone and tea on the coffee table. Settling back in the plush cushions, she stared out the window. The rain had stopped and the sun was out shining brightly, but there wasn't a single bright spot in Teyona's world.

Teyona's phone rang. She glanced over at it and saw that it was Russell calling. She picked it up. "Hello," she answered.

"I'm so glad you answered this time. I was worried about you," he said.

"I'm sorry."

"Don't be sorry," he said and asked, "I'm just checking to see if you're okay. Are you okay?"

"I really couldn't say. Right now I'm numb. I just feel like I'm existing."

"I understand. What you just went through was traumatic and it will take some time to recover but it's gonna happen." He'd already seen her enormous strength and knew that if anyone could overcome all that'd happened, it was she. "It's all gonna be alright. I know it will," he said with such conviction that a small smile touched the corners of her mouth, but she didn't comment.

"Do you need anything?"

"No, I'm fine."

"Are you sure?"

"Yes."

"Neither of us had anything to eat last night and you wouldn't have breakfast with me this morning when I asked you. What have you eaten since yesterday?"

Teyona didn't answer him.

"You haven't eaten anything, have you?"

"I tried but I must have lost my appetite."

"You have to eat. I'm bringing you something," he offered. "I take it your husband is not around."

"No, he is not and no, I don't want you to bring me anything."

Without asking any further questions about Steven, instead, Russell said, "I'll be there within the hour."

"No, please, don't do that. I really don't have much of an appetite. I will probably feel more like having something tomorrow," she said but when he didn't respond, she looked at the face of her phone and realized he'd already hung up.

Almost immediately, her phone rang again. Without checking the identity of the called, she answered. "Look, I appreciate your checking on me but I don't want you to bring me anything. I'm going to be. . ."

"Teyona, this is Steven," he said, interrupting her. "Who were you expecting a call from?"

Ignoring his question, she snapped, "What do you want, Steven?"

"I just wanted to see if you're alright."

"So now you want to know whether I'm alright. Were you concerned about me when you were banging all those other women? Were you concerned about me then? I don't think so."

He stated quietly, "You know this is the first time since we've been together that we didn't spend our Saturday together."

Teyona didn't respond.

"How do you feel about that? I know you've thought of it because I've been thinking about it all day." When Teyona still didn't respond, he said, "I was wondering if I could come over tomorrow so we can talk."

"We've already had that talk, Steven so you coming over here would be just a waste of time and I have no more time left to waste on you."

"Teyona, you know people make mistakes and I made a number of them, but I don't want to lose all that we've accomplished because I've been a low life. I love you and want to spend the rest of my life with you. I know you love me too, Teyona, I know you do. The kind of love you and I share is too powerful to throw away. That's the kind of love that lasts a lifetime. Don't you agree?"

"Goodnight, Steven," she said ending the call. When her phone rang again, she reached over, shut off the ringer and reclined back in the chair where she began to revisit the past twenty-four hours. One minute, she and Steven had everything going for themselves; they had been in love, they were successful with wonderful careers, they were respected in their community, they had a wonderful family, and the next, her entire life had been turned upside down.

Twenty minutes later, the sound of her doorbell brought her out of her thoughts. Reclining further in the chair, she tried to ignore it, hoping whoever was at her door would go away. The bell rang again. She slowly got up from the couch and walked down the hall to see who the visitor was.

She flung opened the door. "What are you doing here?"

Russell was carrying two brown paper bags in his hands. He said, "Show me to the kitchen, please."

Russell was more handsome than Teyona ever remembered. He was wearing a tan, short sleeve pullover and brown slacks and shoes. A slow, small smile curved his beautifully shaped lips at seeing her. Looking at him and shaking her head, she stood back and allowed him to enter, acutely aware that she was only wearing a flimsy nightgown.

"I told you I didn't want anything," she said.

"I know," he said, crossing over the threshold.

Closing the door behind him as they went to the kitchen together she asked, "What have you got there?" In the kitchen, Russell set the bags on the counter, removed the containers and set them on the table. He went over to pulled utensils from a drawer, a plate from the cabinet above the sink and a dish of butter from the refrigerator before returning to the table. He emptied the bagels on the plate, handed Teyona a soup spoon and he set containers of hot tea with lemon on the table for them before he sat to have his bagel and soup.

Teyona spooned some of the soup into her mouth. "Umm, this is delicious." She glanced over at Russell. "I didn't realize I was so hungry."

"I'm glad that you are eating something. You have to eat to keep your strength up and right now, you need all your strength." He looked concerned and asked, "Have you talked with your husband or your friend?"

"Yes, I talked with Steven. It's the reason he's not here right now."

"What did he have to say for himself?"

"The usual things I would imagine men say when they've been caught doing something wrong and doesn't want to lose what they have."

"Nothing from Rachelle, huh?"

"No, nothing yet. Anyway, what can she say? I have a feeling she couldn't care less about what they've done."

"You think she will call?" Russell asked, biting off a piece of bagel and spooning soup into his mouth.

"Yeah," she answered. "I'm sure she will after some time has passed."

"What are you gonna say to her? Just keep in mind that the woman is a cold hearted bitch. She doesn't care about anything but herself and that is just one of many things that make her dangerous."

"I don't care how dangerous she is. I'd just like to put my foot in her ass." Teyona shook her head, then added, "I don't know. I can only say with certainty is that I will never trust her again. Neither of them." Not wanting to talk anymore about Steven or Rachelle, Teyona changed the subject. "Have you thought any more about when you are leaving Columbia?"

"As you know, my business here is about finished but I'm not ready to put this town behind yet," he said, and added, looking at her over his tea container as he sipped from it, "I definitely don't want to leave you."

Teyona didn't respond to his comment. She just gazed at him from across the table.

Wiping her mouth with the paper napkin that Russell had placed on the table by her plate, she acknowledged, "That was great. Thank you so much."

"Oh, you don't have to thank me. I'm just glad that you were able to eat a little something."

Abruptly, Teyona rose out of her seat. "I appreciate what you've done for me but I think you should leave now."

Russell looked up at her before getting up from his seat. "Okay," he said although he wasn't ready to leave her just yet. In such a short time, he'd become so smitten with her. If he had his way, he'd stay with her—forever. "I'll check on you tomorrow, if that's alright."

She nodded her consent. He took her hand as she led him to the front door, his feet echoed on the hardwood floor, piercing the silence. At the door, she placed her hand on the knob to open the door for him. He laid his hand on top of hers. She turned to look at him, their eyes gazed into each other's and slowly, his arms went around her trim waist. He pulled her to him, her arms immediately went up around his neck and she raised her mouth to his. Tongues teasing and dueling, their kiss growing intensely, as they fiercely caressed each other. Russell tore his mouth from hers, kissing her face, down her neck, the hollow of her throat. He slipped his hand beneath the soft fabric of her robe to capture one of her breast.

Lowering his head, he flicked his tongue around her nipple, encircling it moments before his mouth clamped down and began to suck fiercely on it with her moaning out loud with pleasure. Reaching down, untying the sash to her robe, he slid it off her shoulders, exposing her full round breasts. His eyes gleamed as they moved down her body, mesmerized that she wasn't wearing anything underneath her robe. Their eyes remained locked, drinking in the depths of each other's need and desire.

Russell's mouth returned to Teyona's and in one easy swoop, he held her in his arms and effortlessly carried her upstairs.

"No, Russell. No," she choked out, her eyes closed, head still spinning from the assault of his mouth on her body moments ago. He entered the first bedroom they came to and he carried her across the room. "No, Russell," she protested again. "No….," she said, but he ignored her protest, her words got lost in his mouth in a kiss that sent them tumbling on the bed together. Teyona tore her mouth from his and for an instant she stared into his intense hazel eyes, completely overwhelmed at what she felt for him, how easy it was to accept love from him and to give her love to him. She pulled his sweater over his head and unzipped his pants. He got her out of her robe, and within moments, they were naked and in each other's arms again, kissing, caressing, groping. Her arms went up around his neck, pulling him closer to her as he moved his hand up and down her body. After a while, he rolled on top of her as she parted her legs for him.

His mouth moved from her lips to her breast again. He gently sucked her nipples, going from one to the other before he took her breasts into his hands and continuing to give them equal treatment, he enclosed his mouth on her and gave her pleasure that sent shutters through her body.

His mouth left her breast and traveled lower on her body. She lifted her leg one moment before she felt his tongue burrowing through her soft intimate curls that were already moistened, and he began to lick at her. He opened his mouth, enclosed it around her feminine spot and there he feasted on her ferociously, giving her phenomenal pleasure filling her mind, body and soul with his fiery, young, powerful spirit, causing her eyes to roll back in her head.

Sometime later, Russell moved from her center, kissing her as he progressed up her body. When their bodies were perfectly aligned, he covered her mouth with his, plundered her mouth with his tongue and kissed her like a man starving for her. She moaned, running her fingers through his hair as he kissed her over and over until she sighed with pleasure and pulled him down atop her. He entered her and as she took him inside, her heart began to race. He thrust in and out of her, picking up the pace all the while. As he skillfully dove deeper and deeper into her, she moved her body vigorously against him and they soared off into timeless space.

They climaxed together, not separating, holding on to each other tightly.

"Are you okay?" He asked,

"Yes, I'm fine. What about you?"

"Oh, I'm great. I couldn't be better." He tucked her closer into his arms, only wanting to love her, protect her and as she felt his heartbeat, she felt love, protection and more, so much more. "I haven't been able to get you out of my mind from the first moment I saw you. I think I was attracted to you at first sight."

"How can you say that when we initially met, you called me names and treated me badly?"

"I know. I was acting on raw emotions. I am so glad I got to know you. You are not gonna believe this but I learned more about my brother through you than I knew before. I've also learned some things about myself, and I know now that it was because of you that Bobby reached out to me and he and I became family again. I still wish he'd come back to Detroit or that I had come here sooner." Russell was quiet for a moment. "When you and I first met, I want you to know that I'm not that guy. I don't have an excuse for me behavior except to say that I was acting out without the benefit of knowledge and I am sorry and I am hoping you will find it in your heart to forgive me. Forgive me for the awful things that I did to you?"

"I understand why you did what you did. Given the same set of circumstances, I am not sure I wouldn't have done some of the same things. We just don't know what we will do or how we will behave if we experience life altering situations."

"I have to know that you forgive me."

"I'll let you know."

CHAPTER 28

RACHELLE

Rachelle left the hotel. A little self-conscious with the bruises she received during her fight with Steven, but very cheerful. It was all out in the open now. Little Ms. Teyona knew everything. Good for the bitch, she thought. Thinking her life was so damn perfect. So what if their friendship was over. It was her time to shine. Teyona had put Steven out and now she was going to do the same to George. That man had been dragging her down since she married him. What a wimp. She was now going to have it all.

Rachelle got in her car and returned home. Coming in the front door, she smelled something wonderful in the kitchen. Well, if there was one good thing about George, it was that man can cook his ass off. She made a beeline to the kitchen, seeing George standing over the open oven removing a dish. He placed the dish on the counter top, removed the mitts, went to the sink and began washing his hands.

Rachelle cleared her throat, announcing her presence. George turned around and said, "Rachelle, I didn't see you there. I was just making dinner. Care for some?"

Despite the wonderful smells, Rachelle declined. "Listen, George, we need to talk."

A worried expression crossed George's face. "What do you want to talk about?" he asked as he picked up a towel to wipe his hands dry.

"There's no easy way to say it," Rachelle began, "Us. We're through."

"What?!" George couldn't believe what he was hearing.

"Do you need me to repeat it for you, George," she snapped. "I said we're through. It's over. I'm filing for a divorce.

"What? Why?" he could hardly stumble out.

"Because," she said cruelly, "you're a poor excuse for a husband, provider and lover."

"Rachelle, where is all of this coming from?" George wanted to know.

She twisted her neck to one side, looking at George like he was crazy. "I am done with you. You were so lucky to get me but now I can finally have the man I desire and love."

"Man you desire and love," he repeated weakly.

"Yes," she replied, smiling wickedly. "It's about time I let you in on a secret. I've been fucking guys on the side for as long as we have been married; here, abroad, wherever I wanted. Since you weren't filling my needs in the bedroom, I had to go outside our marriage. But, that's not all, Sweetheart," she went in for the kill, "I've been fucking Dr., Steven Carter."

"Steven?" George looked crestfallen.

"Yes, Steven," she confirmed. She went up to George, playfully tracing a finger down his chest. "And, you remember when I went to Mama's a while back," she began. "George's eyes grew wide. "Um hum, I wasn't suffering from stress at work." She looked dead into George's eyes. "I was pregnant with Steven's child." George immediately tensed up. "Steven and I have a beautiful baby boy together," she cooed.

Cool, laid back George roughly grabbed Rachelle. "I forgave you when I found out you had cheated on me before because I loved you, but you have not only been cheating on me with different men, you've been screwing my friend Steven and your friend Teyona's husband."

Rachelle answered, "Um hum," smiling brightly. "Let me give you all the details…" Rachelle filled George in to all her sexual escapades up to the men she'd slept with in the Bahamas and of course her trysts with Steven. Then, she told George to pack his things and get out which he was all but too happy to.

Later, George came down the stairs with his suitcase, finding Rachelle calmly stuffing her face at the kitchen table with the dinner he'd prepared. Their eyes met and she daintily forked some roast into her mouth. "Bye, bye," she purred, feeling more pleased with herself than she had in months.

"Oh and George," she waved the fork at him, "Dinner was delicious."

"I hope you choke on it, bitch," George growled, turned and walked out the door.

CHAPTER 29

TEYONA

On Sunday morning, Teyona picked up the newspaper from her front step. She opened the paper as she turned to re-enter the house and her eyes flew wide open and a hand flew to her mouth. The headline screamed of a murder in an upscale neighborhood and there was a picture of Rachelle. She was the victim.

"Oh my goodness," Teyona said. She was angry at Rachelle and wanted her to hurt as much as she and Steven had hurt her but she didn't want to see her dead. She immediately thought about George. Did he know what she and Steven had done? She ran to her phone and called George's cell.

George picked up after three rings. "Hello," he answered groggily.

"George, it's Teyona. Are you all right?" she asked.

"No, Teyona." George confessed, "I just found out last night that my wife had been cheating on me with several different men and your husband.

279

"You found out last night?" Teyona quizzed. "George, please don't tell me," she began.

"Don't tell you what?" he asked, confused. "Rachelle gleefully told me all about her cheating, then she threw me out. Bitch even took the time to eat the meal I spent all day preparing," he growled.

"George, where are you?"

"I'm where I been all night, since she put me out." He gave Teyona the name of the hotel he was staying at.

"Have you been there all night?" Teyona asked, hoping that he had an alibi for Rachelle's murder.

"Well, no, I did stop off at Jimmy's and had a few drinks before going to the hotel. I feel like such a fool." He punched his fist into a pillow.

"I know how you feel, but you were trusting just like I was. No one ever thinks their love one and best friend would do what Rachelle and Steven did to us," Teyona said softly.

"I tried. I tried so hard to be and do everything she wanted, but it was never enough for her," George said. "Even after she cheated, I tried to work it out. I know there was distance between us. I tried to ignore that distance that was constantly growing between us but instead of things getting better, the distance became so great until the distance was all we had." He paused a moment. "Why did she stay with me if she didn't want me, if she despised me so?" he asked Teyona and she could hear the tremendous pain in his voice.

"You can never decipher someone's motives. Some people are just cruel and uncaring."

280

"Yeah, well that bitch will never be uncaring to me again. I made sure of that.

Teyona's head jerked up. "What do you mean by that, George?" she asked but George's line dropped.

Teyona got up, panicking. Could George have killed Rachelle? He was certainly angry enough and all the abuse he took from Rachelle. It would have sent any man over the edge. Maybe Rachelle finally found George's breaking point. She didn't want to believe her friend could kill Rachelle. George had so much going for himself and he was such a good man.

She called Russell. When he answered, she blurted out, "Russell, Rachelle's dead and I think George may have killed her."

CHAPTER 30

TEYONA, RUSSELL & STEVEN

Russell received Teyona's frantic call and rushed right over to her house. She threw the door open before Russell made it up the front steps.

"Here, look," she thrust the paper into Russell's hands. "Rachelle was murdered last night. I called George and he told me that Rachelle had confessed everything to him. The many men she cheated on him with, even her son with Steven."

Russell took Teyona's hands in his. "Calm down," he stated. "We need to think things through clearly." Teyona quieted and took some deep breaths while Russell read the article concerning Rachelle's murder.

Russell's detective skills started working. "Of course, the police are going to look at George first," he explained to Teyona, "because in instances like these, it's usually the jilted spouse."

Teyona reacted with horror. "No, I know George. He's a real good man. He's hurt but he couldn't harm a fly."

Russell looked at her in disbelief. "You mean like you thought you knew your husband and your best friend?" Attempting to ask Teyona gently, he saw the almost imperceptible flinch, knowing he'd stuck a raw nerve.

"You're right," she stated, head cast down. "I guess I don't know people as well as I think I do."

Russell leaned over, taking Teyona in his arms. "I'm sorry. I didn't say what I said to hurt you. I just meant the truth is that we really don't know what someone is capable of. Especially those close to us." He leaned back and looked into her face. "Let me take a look at this situation and see what's going on. I promise you, we will know something and soon," he assured her.

Teyona snuggled in Russell's arms, sobs beginning to form when, all of a sudden they were confronted by a wild-eyes and intoxicated Steven who charged at Russell from across the room.

"You son-of-a-bitch," Steven roared. "You're the motherfucker that ruined my marriage, destroyed my life." Russell shoved Teyona away from him. Standing up, he confronted Steven head on. Steven threw a right punch which Russell easily blocked and hit Steven with an uppercut. Steven fell hard on his ass.

"Steven, leave," Teyona screamed. "I told you to not come back here without letting me know."

Steven turned to Teyona. "You bitch, I bet you were fucking him, too." Then he directed his attention to Russell. "I told your brother I would stuff his balls down his throat for messing with my wife and I'll do the same to you too." He got back up to his feet and rushed Russell again.

Russell backed hand him on his ass. "We can play this game all day, Pops," Russell said, "but the lady would like you to leave. And, the only person that ruined your marriage is you, Steven. You were the one cheating with all the different women and Rachelle, your wife's best friend."

Steven's face twitched on the mention of Rachelle. He looked over at Teyona and asked, "Did you know," Steven nodded his head towards Russell, "he had Rachelle helping him to scare you?" he questioned Teyona. "Huh, did you know that about your little boy toy?"

Teyona met Steven's gaze. "Russell took responsibility for everything he did. Unlike you, he told me everything. Now, I want you to leave. Russell, please remove this man from my home," she turned to Russell.

Russell went over to Steven. As he did, Steven quickly rose to his feet and brandished a gun. Gazing at Russell, he said, "No motherfucker, I ain't going nowhere." Then, to Teyona, "but your little fuck buddy is." He cocked the gun. "Get over there, he kept the gun on Russell but motioned Teyona to his side.

"Please, Steven, don't do this," Teyona begged.

"Shut up. I don't want to hear you begging for this lowlife?"

He strode up to Russell, feeling more powerful with the cold, deadly piece of steel in his hand. "I had everything just the way I wanted; a devoted

284

wife and plenty of women to satisfy me on the side." He turned to Teyona. "Oh, you satisfied me completely, but once was just never enough," he said, smiling boyishly at her. He continued, looking back at Russell. "You brought your ass into my home, sat, talked to my wife, all the while, you planned to screw up my marriage." He held the gun tighter.

"No," Russell said, "I didn't come here to mess up your marriage. I came here to make someone pay for killing my brother. I watched you and from the beginning, I thought you were Mr. Perfect and that your wife had royally screwed you over until I caught your act with your nurse and then, I ran into Rachelle."

Again, Steven flinched upon hearing Rachelle's name. "Rachelle, Rachelle! Everything goes back to that bitch," he exploded.

Slowly, Teyona backed away from Steven. "Steven," she said, quietly.

Steven turned wild eyes on to her. "That bitch, Rachelle," he roared, "she's the cause of all this. I never should have gotten involved with her." Tears began forming in his eyes but he held the gun steady focused on Russell. "My biggest mistake was getting involved with her. The bitch was so dogged. She pursued me until I couldn't resist. It was like she knew my weakness. We hook up and then she got pregnant. She went to her mother's house in North Carolina, to have the baby and came back home. I was paying her mother and her mother's neighbor to help care for the child. Things

285

were going fine until she came to me, telling me that her mother was unable to care for the child any longer. Neither was her neighbor. I told her to do whatever she needed to do to keep the child in North Carolina, that I would pay for it but she lied and brought the boy to Columbia."

Teyona stared at Steven. She'd known most of the story. Russell had told her but she didn't know Rachelle had brought the child to Columbia.

"Where's the child, Steven?" she asked.

"Rachelle said he was with a friend," he answered, unconcerned. "It's not like I gave a damn anymore," he said.

Teyona's eyes grew wide. "What do you mean? You don't care about your son?" she stared at him disbelievingly.

"I don't care because that lying bitch, Rachelle lied," he bellowed. "I went over to George and Rachelle's with the intention of confessing everything to George. I meant to apologize to him for the wrong I had done to him but I found Rachelle there and she told me she'd put him out. I demanded to know where the boy was so I smacked her around until she told me. She went and got George's gun and said she was gonna shoot me if I struck her again. Can you believe that shit?" he asked more to himself. "We fought over the gun, it fired and struck her. She was mortally wounded so there wasn't anything I could do other than make her comfortable, but she died. Now get this, before she died, she confessed that Stevie Jr. wasn't my son. He is actually George's son. Initially, she had

286

decided to make the best of the situation and finger me as the father and I believed her." Tears began to flow freely from his eyes. "I am so sorry, Teyona. I never meant for any of this to happen." He fell to his knees and started sobbing like a child. "I'm so sorry. I'm so sorry," he wailed over and over like a mantra.

Russell rushed over and snatched the gun from his hand. He used his phone to call the police. Officers quickly arrived and arrested Steven who was still sobbing even as he was led away in cuffs. Officers took statements from Teyona and Russell. They informed Teyona that they had broke the news of Rachelle's murder to George and he'd been devastated. Russell provided them with a copy of Steven's confession he'd surreptitiously recorded on his phone. After the officers left, Teyona and Russell talked.

"I can't believe Steven killed Rachelle," Teyona mused. "That's so unlike him."

"He will probably get probation. It was accidental and he's very remorseful," Russell offered.

Teyona shook her head. "Rachelle played with fire and got burned. At least she lived her life to the fullest. She did it her way. Oh, I need to tell George about his son," she smiled.

"It appears that all I need to do now is locate where the boy is being kept and get a DNA just to be certain that everything is on the up and up. Give me a few days," Russell said.

"Won't George be surprised if in fact the child is his? I can see him now. He's gonna need a lot of help with the boy especially with his startup company just beginning."

This time it was Russell who shook his head. "There you go, always thinking about others."

CHAPTER 31

TEYONA & GEORGE

Two days after Rachelle's funeral, Teyona left Russell and Stevie Jr. in her car. Russell had been able to find out which of Rachelle's friends was taking care of her son, where she lived and she released the boy to Russell and after the appropriate test was done, he took the baby to Teyona's house.

Teyona was excited as she walked up the sidewalk and rung the doorbell at George's house. His sister answered the door.

"Thank you for the lovely flowers and all that you did in helping us through this terrible situation," Tracey said to Teyona.

"Absolutely, Tracey. This has been difficult for everyone, but please let me know if there's anything else I can do for you all," Teyona replied as Tracey showed her into the living room where George was sitting with several other visitors. Her heart broke when she saw George; he looked lost, completely devastated. His eyes were bloodshot; whether from lack of sleep, excessive drinking or the recent losses he had experienced. Seeing Teyona, George's face brightened a little, he got up from his seat and the two of them embraced each other. After expressing condolences to George and his family, together she and George walked across the hall to the library.

"I didn't want to bring this up before but I think now is a good time that I share something very special with you," Teyona began and she watched a puzzled expression cover George's face. She continued talking and didn't stop until she'd told him everything he didn't already know about Rachelle and Steven. With a look of incredulity on his face, Teyona and George embraced and she rushed out of the house, leaving a stunned George standing in the doorway. Minutes later, she returned carrying a little boy in her arms and a bag hanging across her shoulder.

George walked down the steps to meet them, never taking his eyes from the little boy's. "George, meet your son," she said, handing him the bag and placing the child's small hand in his. After a moment, Teyona left them and returned to her car and to a waiting Russell as George returned to his house, carrying his son in his arms and closed the door behind them.

When Teyona heard from George again, he told her he'd hired a nanny to care for his son and an attorney who'd handle the necessary paperwork to change the baby's name from Steven Carter, Jr. to Christopher Devin Marchant, after George's father. Teyona knew that George had a long difficult road ahead before all the pain and heartache subsided due to what his wife and friend put him through, but she also knew that little Christopher would make that journey so much easier.

CHAPTER 32

TEYONA & RUSSELL

Teyona hadn't spoken to Steven since the day he was removed from their home by the police but she'd seen in the papers that he'd been released from jail and had returned to his medical practice. She was glad for him and hoped that he'd learned something from the unwise choices he'd made.

She packed her suitcases and brought them downstairs. Russell looked up from where he'd been sitting when she entered the den. He got up and walked over to her as she set the suitcases on the floor.

"So you're going to be living in Charleston for a while, huh?"

"Yeah. I just need to get away for a while and allow myself to heal before I decide what I want to do with the rest of my life."

"I understand," was all Russell had said but she already knew he didn't want her to leave town without him yet he knew she was doing what she had to do. She needed the time and space to process all the changes that had occurred in her life. Somewhere inside, Russell knew he would never, could never mean to Teyona what she meant to him, but he would always be grateful for the moments they shared. "I hope after you've healed sufficiently and you need an old friend to talk to, I hope you will contact me."

Teyona smiled at him and took a deep breath. "I can't say what I will do today, tomorrow or five years from now, Russell. But, I want to thank you for everything you did for me. I don't know what I would have done without you and there will always be a special place in my heart for you." She reached out and caught his hands. "And, for what it's worth, I do forgive you, Russell, I do but right now, that's all I can give you."

Russell placed Teyona's bags into the trunk of her car, she got into her car and as she started the engine, Russell felt more pain in his heart than anyone had a right to feel. He wondered if he'd ever see Teyona again. Would she go on with her life without him, would he be forced to go on with his without her? He didn't have the answer. But, one thing he knew for sure. He loved Teyona and he knew he'd never love anyone else the way he loved her.

Russell closed the door to her car and he bent to say a last goodbye to her. Through the open car window, Teyona allowed her lips to brush Russell's ever so lightly. "Take care of yourself, will you?" she whispered.

"And you as well," he replied and after giving her one last longing look, he walked away to get into his car.

Recently, Teyona had experienced some devastating losses and through it all, she knew they weren't just the end of something, they were the beginning of something else, whatever that may be. She would take this time to make some assessment, reexamine her life because an unexamined life was not worth living and she knew she had a lot to live for.

Teyona gave Russell a small smile as they waved goodbye to each other. He followed her out of her driveway and down to the end of the street that intercepted with Forest Drive. There, she turned left, he turned right and they drove off in different directions, continuing their journey.